To Olivi
With tha

Harry.

March 2019

SHROUD THE TRUTH

WITH

SILENCE

HARRY WATERMAN

Acknowledgements

My sincere thanks to the following people for their time and their valued contributions to the writing of this novel; it was greatly appreciated:

Kevin Green
Doug Galloway
Chris Sheppard
Dr. Sarah Fawcett

This book is dedicated to the memory of
Martin Evans

RIP my dear friend

Shroud The Truth With Silence

There is an evil which I have seen under the sun,
and it is common among men
Ecclesiastes Chapter 6

Shroud The Truth With Silence

The Day of the Murder

(Tuesday, September 30, 1952)

Headlines in the South Wales Argus (Evening Edition):

—Local Doctor Brutally Murdered!—

At approximately 3.00pm today hospital staff at the newly formed Llanarth Court Secure Mental Institution, near Raglan, found the body of Dr. Anthony Weldon in his second-floor office. Initial reports indicate that the doctor had been stabbed.

The deceased was Head of Department at the hospital and a highly respected practitioner according to the staff there: Clinical Psychologist, Phillip Manson, who worked closely with Dr. Weldon was today quoted as saying:

"The whole department is deeply shocked by this tragic incident. It's hard to believe something like this could happen here. Without a doubt, Doctor Weldon will be sorely missed."

Latest News—Female Employee Arrested

A 20-year-old female employee at the hospital has been arrested on suspicion of murder and taken into police custody in Newport...

*

From the moment hospital staff discovered Vera Parsons slumped over the doctor's body, she fell silent and she did not speak another word for nearly fifteen years. Consequently, she was unable—or unwilling, to plead guilty—or not guilty, in a court of law and was therefore unable to be tried for murder, which at that time carried the death penalty by hanging.

Instead, Vera Parsons was sent to a secure mental institution near London, where she remained incarcerated, until her eventual release in 1970 after being assessed by the Parole Board as:

"No longer a threat to the community at large."

Shroud The Truth
With Silence

Shroud The Truth With Silence

Chapter 1

I did what I had to do

Cambridge, England
(Present day)

Why has this murder never been solved? Melanie Underwood pondered, as she turned left off the main road at the T-junction.

The young criminal psychologist was preoccupied, deep in thought—mulling over the evidence against Vera Parsons, the old lady she was about meet, face-to-face; but she was struggling to crystallise her thoughts and make sense of the details in the SIO's case notes.

Was she protecting someone by staying silent for all of those years—banged up in a mind-numbing mental institution—or was she simply protecting herself? Either way, it worked, Melanie reminded herself, *because nobody has ever been charged with the murder and Vera Parsons avoided the gallows—even though she was found slumped on top of the doctor's body with her fingerprints all over the murder weapon.* Melanie recalled the case details she'd been reading before she left the office. *And don't forget,* she reminded herself, *she's never been officially charged with any offence at all!*

I wonder if she'll open up to what really happened that day? But then again, girl, why should she? If she did kill the doctor she's hardly likely to admit it to you, is she?

Melanie pondered:

She's never explained to anyone what really happened—and she must be in her late-eighties now.

God! She was just a kid in 1952 when they arrested her on suspicion of murder.

So if she didn't do it, then maybe she knows who did —but that would mean she's been protecting a murderer for most of her life.

So why would she protect someone who killed her lover?—That, Melanie, makes no sense at all.

I need to get into her head. I need to understand what really happened that day.

Some three-hundred-yards down the leafy tree-lined road, Melanie Underwood indicated and turned right into a small carpark, deftly slotting her Mini Cooper into the last remaining visitor's parking space.

That was lucky, she thought, as she switched off the engine and checked her watch. 'Eighteen minutes from the office; that's not bad for Cambridge at this time of the day.' She then checked her makeup in the driver's mirror before stepping out of the car and walking the short distance to the nursing home's main entrance. She glanced up at a black and white sign near the door that said:

Welcome to the Grange

Residential Nursing Home

(Specialists in Dementia Care)

The once splendid Edwardian house now served as a home for some thirty-or-so elderly residents and was funded in part by the local council.

Melanie smiled. 'Here we go then,' she said, somewhat hesitantly. As she approached the entrance, her boss's words of advice returned to her mind:

Don't raise your hopes too high, young lady, you'll only be disappointed.

Melanie knew how much this opportunity meant to her and she knew she'd only get one chance to find out what really happened the day Vera Parsons's lover, Doctor Anthony Weldon, was murdered.

She was feeling nervous but tried hard not to show it; she took a few deep breaths to calm herself.

'I'll show you, Alan Cornish,' she said, defiantly.

I wonder what she'll be like? Will she like me? I hope she's not a cantankerous old biddy whose hearing-aid batteries need changing. Stay calm girl, stay calm.

'You must be Miss Underwood?' said a rotund woman standing outside the main door, smoking a cigarette.

Melanie smiled nervously as she walked up the steps towards her. 'Yes, I'm Miss Underwood,' she replied, raising her ID card for the woman to see.

'We've been expecting you…Criminal Psychologist. *Bloody hell!*—I've not met one of them before,' she said, excitedly, as they shook hands. 'Carol's the name, by the way.'

'Pleased to meet you, Carol.'

'Has Vera robbed a bank or something?' the carer asked, as she pushed her cigarette butt into a sand tray.

Melanie smiled. *So they don't know about her past,* she thought, and made a mental note.

'Vera's in the day lounge, Miss Underwood; follow me and I'll take you through. The old girl doesn't get many visitors, so she'll probably enjoy having someone *sensible* to talk to—if you know what I mean… She's

4

not in any kind of trouble is she?' the carer asked, discreetly.

'No, not at all,' Melanie replied.

'Good—because she can be a bit cantankerous when she wants to be.'

Oh God! Just my luck, Melanie thought, forcing a weak smile.

Halfway down a tired looking hallway that smelt of disinfectant the carer showed Melanie through some double-doors into a large sunlit room. Inside, elderly men and women occupied high-backed chairs arranged around the perimeter of the cheaply carpeted lounge. The air in the room was stale and acrid and it was uncomfortably warm.

Melanie's reaction was to cringe as she walked in. *God—this is awful!*

'Vera—Miss Underwood is here.'

Melanie watched as the carer wagged her finger at the diminutive figure sitting in an armchair facing the windows.

'Make sure you behave yourself, you hear me? If you don't you'll be in trouble again my girl, do you understand?' Before leaving, the carer pulled up a conference chair next to the old lady and invited Melanie to sit down. The young psychologist felt somewhat self-conscious; aware that all around the room squinting eyes were scrutinising her.

Holding out her hand, Melanie said:

'It's lovely to meet you, Miss Parsons, I'm very grateful to you for seeing me.'

The frail old lady, dressed in a floral pink frock, heavy-denier winter stockings and open-toed sandals, pointed a cadaverous finger at an equally gaunt looking woman sitting on the opposite side of the room.

'She thinks I'm mad—but *that* mindless old cow sits there all bloody day staring out of the window, muttering to herself, farting and stinking of piss. If they took her cushions away the daft bitch would keel over like a sailboat in a storm. Who is *she* to say *I'm* mad? Anyway, I'm glad to announce she's wearing her death mask today. She's not long for this world, take my word for it; I know more than most people about *life*... and *death*.' The old lady pouted her bottom lip and nodded her head, giving additional credence to her stage-whispered prophecy.

The young psychologist had to agree with Vera Parsons's prognosis when she glanced across at the vampire-white face and sunken eyes staring straight through her.

'Why does she think you're mad, Miss Parsons?' Melanie asked, inquisitively.

The old lady smiled to herself for some time in pensive silence. Eventually, she answered:

'Young lady, *everyone* here thinks I'm mad!'

'Why is that?'

Vera Parsons tensed and clenched the arms of her chair. '…Because.'

'You mean *because* of what you did, Miss Parsons?' the psychologist tentatively asked.

Vera laughed and Melanie responded with a nervous smile.

'…Fuck you!' Vera yelled, venomously.

Melanie Underwood stiffened and dropped her pen in shock. *This is not going well,* she quickly realised.

Chapter 2

So, what's your theory Miss, Criminal Psychologist,
Underwood?

'VERA!—language!' came the
chastisement from a female voice somewhere outside
the room.

The old lady smirked contentedly and said, coldly:

'I know why you're here. You're here to tell them
that I'm still *insane*. Well, let me tell you something
young lady—I don't give a shit what *you* or *they* think,'
she said, with a dismissive wave of her hand. 'I did
what I had to do.'

Melanie picked up her pen from the carpet and
struggled to compose herself; clearly perturbed by
Vera's unexpected outburst, which raised a number of
the resident's eyebrows and instigated a flurry of gasps
and giggles around the room.

'…I'm sorry if you think that, Miss Parsons, but that's not why I'm here, I can *assure* you. I'm here to hopefully understand what really happened on that fateful day.'

The old lady regarded her young visitor with suspicious eyes. '…Why do you care what happened *on that fateful day* as you put it? You weren't even born.'

'Do you really want to take your secret to the grave Miss Parsons? Unless of course you really did murder Doctor Weldon.' Melanie regretted the words as they escaped from her lips. '…I'm sorry, Miss Parsons, I shouldn't have said that.'

Shit! Shit! Shit!

'So, what's your theory Miss, *Criminal Psychologist,* Underwood? What do you think happened on that—fateful day?'

The expectant audience fell silent as Melanie wrestled with the old lady's question. She felt suddenly faint.

'Well?… We're all waiting,' Vera urged, smugly.

Oh God! What do I say? Melanie took a deep breath; her mind was in turmoil.

Vera continued to press…'Well?'

Melanie straightened her back and inhaled. '…You…You… found out that your lover was cheating on you and in a fit of rage you killed him!' *Oh, fuck!*

Vera nodded and smiled. 'Go on,' she urged her visitor.

Melanie took another breath, struggling to find a morsel of composure. A bead of perspiration trickled into her cleavage like a tear. '…You realised what you'd done and that you would hang for it.'

Gasps of astonishment filled the room.

Vera mimicked a noose around her neck and stuck out her tongue.

The gasps changed to laughter.

Melanie continued. '…So you decided to remain silent. That meant you couldn't plead guilty, or not guilty, in a court of law, and therefore you could not be tried for murder. You killed your lover and very *cleverly* avoided the hangman.' Melanie looked deflated. *Oh Christ—I've blown it now!*

'So that's your theory is it, young lady?' Vera asked, smiling.

Melanie replied, defiantly:

'Yes—yes, it is.'

Vera Parsons was infatuated with Melanie Underwood's beautiful young face, near perfect, slightly flushed complexion and vibrant green eyes. For a while she gazed at Melanie in silence but eventually she said:

'Are you going to sit down or do you have piles?'

'…Yes, I mean no, …thank you.' Melanie settled on the conference chair next to the old woman as laughter rippled around the room again.

'… There is a beautiful innocence in your face young lady, but there is also determination and resolve. I admire that. I looked very much like you when I was your age—and look at me now, a wrinkled, white-haired old hag—sitting in God's waiting room.' Vera then touched her breasts. 'And look what gravity has done to my prized assets! They were like yours once!'

Melanie chuckled. *I don't want to get old, she thought.*

'…Looking at you is like turning back the hands of time. You're a breath of fresh air in this awful place.'

Melanie managed a weak smile.

'You're nervous aren't you my dear?' Vera asked, softly, glancing down at the young woman's trembling hands.

'Yes—I am a bit, Miss Parsons,' Melanie admitted.

'How I envy you young girl, but please—*stop* calling me Miss *fucking* Parsons. Vera will do nicely, thank you.'

That's a start, thought Melanie, smiling at the capricious old lady's instruction.

Vera's tone softened. 'You really are quite sweet.'

Melanie began to relax. 'I don't think you're insane Vera.'

'But you're a psychologist my dear, not a bloody psychiatrist. There is a difference!'

The old lady's sharp rebuff took Melanie by surprise and put her on edge again.

Vera gestured to the residents with a dismissive wave of her hand. '...This *fucking* lot are convinced I'm mad,' she said.

Melanie glanced around at the collection of shocked faces.

What have I got to lose? Go on—say it. '...But surely they're not *all* psychiatrists, are they?' she retorted.

'Oh—*touché!*—I do like you, Melanie, you've got *spirit!*'

A stooped old man shuffled past them towards the doors; an unlit cigarette balanced precariously between his stiff, nicotine-stained fingers.

Vera watched him as he passed behind her visitor. 'He stinks of piss too,' she said, crinkling her nose in disgust. 'Off for some fresh air, George?' she called out after him.

'Aye,' replied the old man as he left the room.

Vera returned her gaze to her visitor. 'So—you really want to know what happened on *that fateful day*?'

'Yes, I do,' responded Melanie. 'I really do.'

'Why should I tell *you*, young lady? I've never told anyone.'

Melanie remembered from the case notes that Vera had not spoken a single word for over fourteen years after the murder...'Yes, I'm aware of that,' she replied... 'Well, to tell you the truth I'm hoping to use your case as part of my PhD in Criminal Psychology. The work involves identifying and classifying the motives that drive people of different *social* backgrounds to commit murder. It's part of something called *Predictive Policing*—it's all the rage at the moment. I came across your file and it fascinated me straight away because there were no obvious motives for murder.'

Vera's wrinkled forehead furrowed in response to Melanie's explanation and she repeated her words:

'No—obvious—motives...But you do think I'm a murderer, do you, young lady?'

Melanie looked uncomfortable and a little flustered. 'Well, I...I want—'

'Okay,' she said, interrupting Melanie. 'I'll tell you…I'll tell you because there's *something* about you that I find very appealing.'

In Melanie, Vera Parsons could see herself as a young woman again and the thought invigorated her frail body.

Vera continued, 'but not here…not in front of these nosey *morons!*'

Melanie beamed with delight, 'I understand… Shall we take a walk in the garden, Vera? It's really quite pleasant outside.' She knew that if she didn't get out of the acrid atmosphere soon she'd puke!

'Don't leave us now!' a disappointed old lady called out from the corner of the room.

Vera ignored her and considered Melanie's offer. '… Yes…that would be nice. I haven't been outside for a few days. Perhaps a bit of sunshine and some fresh air will do me good.'

Melanie's relief was visible as she offered her arm to the old lady.

With a little help from Melanie, Vera got slowly to her feet and took a deep breath before exclaiming out loud:

'I'm going outside where you *FUCKERS* can't hear me!'

'Vera!' came the chastisement again from the faceless voice somewhere in the building.

As they walked slowly arm-in-arm together down the corridor, Vera said:

'Old age is not like a dinner party or a bottle of fine wine you can share with friends, old age is something you have to bear alone. But *loneliness* is something I got used to a long time ago, because they don't hang the *insane*, do they young lady? They just lock them away and fill them full of mind-bending drugs to serve their penance.'

'They don't hang anyone anymore, Vera.'

Vera stopped in her tracks. '…Have you ever wondered what it must have been like to have the noose placed around your neck? Knowing that in a matter of *seconds* your neck was going to *snap* like a carrot. What would you be thinking my dear?'

Melanie flinched at the thought. 'I'd rather not think about it if you don't mind,' she answered, as they began walking again.

The old lady continued, 'Do you know how many people we hanged in this country, my dear?'

'I'm afraid I don't.'

Vera stopped and looked at Melanie. 'We hanged some eight-hundred, men and women, between 1900 and 1964. Some, they say, had to be carried to the gallows, some soiled themselves as the hood was placed over their heads, some prayed out loud, some sobbed like a child and—some—walked in silent dignity—as if they'd accepted their impending death and felt no fear. I often wonder how many of those poor souls were actually innocent of their crimes?' Vera continued walking arm-in-arm with Melanie. 'I've thought about the different kinds of death penalty, but I'm not sure which one I'd prefer if I had to choose. I suppose a bullet through the heart is the quickest...I don't fancy being cooked in the electric chair... I wonder—when they cut your head off, can you still see as they hold your head up—as a trophy—to appease the baying crowd? I suspect you *can* see them and *hear* them all cheering for a brief moment, after you've been decapitated? What do you think, my dear?'

Melanie cringed and a cold shiver rippled down her spine, but she offered no comment.

Vera continued:

'I remember reading about a French prisoner who'd been decapitated at the guillotine in 1905. A physician, Doctor Beaurieux, present at the execution, noted that after the decapitation if he called out the prisoner's name he opened his eyes. This happened twice, over a matter of thirty-seconds...Fascinating isn't it, actually *knowing* your head had been cut off!'

How bloody morbid! This woman seems obsessed with death! Melanie thought, as they walked out into the sunshine.

'…If they did hang me now I wouldn't care. They'd be doing me a favour to be honest.'

'I can assure you, Vera, that is not going to happen.'

Vera smiled. 'I know, but this world holds nothing of interest for me anymore. I've had my time. My life has become mundane and *meaningless*; this is your world now—to enjoy… Do you have a young man, Melanie?' Vera asked inquisitively.

Melanie responded, happy to change the subject:

'Not at the moment, Vera; I must admit my love-life to date has been a bit of a damp squib.'

'I'm sure that someone as beautiful as you will soon have Mister Right knocking on your door.'

'That's very kind of you to say so…but I'm not in any rush at the moment. I've decided to put all my energy into my career.'

The rear garden was a pleasant place with lots of leafy shade, colourful flowerbeds and a long, well-kept, rectangular lawn. The welcome smell of freshly cut grass lingered in the warm air. At the far end of the lawn was a sturdy oak bench and Melanie and Vera strolled arm-in-arm in silence across the soft lawn towards it. Moments later they settled down next to each other on the bench. The faint drone of distant traffic on the M11 was the only sound to invade the tranquility of the surroundings but soon that was forgotten.

For some time neither of them spoke; silently enjoying the warm sun on their faces and breathing in the flower-scented air.

Then Melanie said:

'I wish I could do more of this. I don't seem to have the time to sit and appreciate the beauty of the world. The flowers smell wonderful, don't they?'

Vera looked at her and nodded. 'Yes, the bees are very busy today. But when you're young and immortal you have far more *important* things than a pretty garden to occupy your mind, my dear. At least it seems that way at the time. But then as you get older you realise immortality was just a cruel illusion of youth. For *some* of us death comes far too soon; and for others *definitely* not soon enough.'

Melanie prompted herself....*Do it now, don't hesitate any longer.* With her heart pounding she asked: 'So what exactly happened at Llanarth Court, Vera?'

The old lady sat up straight, took a deep breath and exhaled loudly. After a brief silence she began:

'...I was just like you once, Melanie, full of vitality with my whole life ahead of me. I appreciate that must be hard for you to imagine as I sit here awaiting the imminent arrival of the Grim Reaper.'

Melanie gave a sympathetic smile and held the old lady's hand.

Vera looked down. 'Even your hand is pretty, young girl.'

Melanie smiled.

Vera continued:

'…You were right to say what you did, my dear, I don't want to take my secrets to the grave with me. Believe me, I've suffered enough heartache in this godless world.' Vera clasped her hands together on her lap and looked at Melanie… 'I'm sure you realise that this is the first time that I've ever talked about what happened all of those years ago?'

Melanie tingled with excitement. 'Yes, I realise that.'

Staring straight ahead, Vera Parsons took a deep breath, and then began to speak, quietly and wittingly:

'…I was a nurse at Llanarth Court in Wales; it was a secure mental hospital, seconded from a monastic order by the newly formed NHS; a beautiful country home it was, miles from anywhere. I can see it now,' she said, fondly, and the old lady's expression brightened. Vera enthused, 'all the men there fancied me, even the patients, God forbid, but I played it cool and it drove them all *wild*—apart from the monks of course,' she added, and giggled like a teenage girl. 'But I didn't care about any of them—except for *one*.' Vera's tone softened. 'I fell in love with him the moment I set eyes on him. I decided I wanted *him* and I went out to get him—But I didn't know then that…'

Melanie watched as the old lady's breathing suddenly laboured and she struggled to catch her breath.

'What didn't you know, Vera?'

Vera began to sob, dabbing her watery eyes with a tissue that she'd pulled from the sleeve of her cardigan.

'I didn't know then that…'

'Vera, it's time for your medication,' came the untimely interruption from the overweight carer striding purposely towards them with a glass of water and a tube of tablets in her hands.

Fuck! Melanie thought.

'At least they can't hear her profanities when she's out here,' the carer said, smirking at Melanie. 'Be careful what you report young lady; Vera has a very, shall we say—*colourful,* imagination.'

'Fuck off, you old cow!'

'Really! I don't have to take this verbal abuse from you. You're so bitter and twisted and just downright *rude*, Vera!' The carer turned and walked away in disgust, emptying the contents of the glass onto the lawn as she marched back towards the main building muttering to herself.

'Fat-arsed bitch!' Vera mumbled.

Melanie waited until the carer was out of sight. 'Please continue, Vera?'

'Yes, I will,' she replied, 'but first—I want to ask you a question.'

'Yes, of course. Go ahead.'

'What is it that makes us what we are?'

Melanie smiled and then answered:

'That's one of the fundamental questions psychologists have been debating forever, Vera; the nature-nurture debate. On the one side, you have the *nativists,* who basically believe everything we do is a product of our inherited genetic code. On the other side, you have the *empiricists,* who believe we start off with a *tabula rasa* or blank slate, and what we become is dependant on what happens to us along the way. Modern thinking tends to be somewhere between the two schools of thought.'

'And what do you think, my dear?'

'Oh, I *definitely* think life shapes and defines us, especially when we're young and our brains are still developing. But don't forget, we are all *individuals* and we all react to life's experiences differently; and maybe that's due to the genetic hand of cards we've been dealt. But, I'm sorry to say, there is no *simple* answer to your question.'

Vera smiled contentedly at Melanie's response. 'Thank you,' she said, 'well at least we both agree. I think you're right, life does shape and define us.'

Melanie asked:

'Are you talking from experience, Vera?'

The old lady looked at Melanie and nodded. 'Yes—I am,' she confirmed.

'…So what was it that happened to you?'

The old lady then began to reveal to Melanie her version of the events that led up to that life-changing day in 1952, when, at just twenty-years-old, she was taken into police custody on suspicion of murder.

Vera smiled. 'I will always remember the day he arrived at Llanarth. It was a Monday—the sixth of August to be precise, 1951. I was only nineteen then and still a virgin. I remember walking across the courtyard when this posh car pulled up at the main entrance. This handsome man in a dark suit got out and lit a cigarette… He was standing there as if he owned the fucking place. *God, h*e was good looking; classic Italian.'

22

Chapter 3

I really don't think I could have been any happier.

'You know the sort, my dear, tall and slim and drop-dead gorgeous, with raven-black, wavy hair.'

Melanie immediately thought of her boss, Alan Cornish, and smiled. 'Yes, I know,' she said.

'Well, he noticed me and gave me a little wave. I nearly wet myself when he came over and said hello. He told me his name was Doctor Anthony Weldon. He then told me that he'd come to work at Llanarth Court. I looked at him with my mouth open, but no bloody words came out, did they? He just grinned at me and walked off. I fell *instantly* in love with him.' Vera sighed. 'I can still remember tingling all over with excitement…We all knew he was coming to replace Doctor Morris but, to be honest, we were expecting some boring-old-fart, because the war had sadly taken a lot our *young* men.' Vera shook her head and said, pensively:

'What a terrible waste of life that bloody war was. All those brave young lads who gave up their *lives* for their country.' Vera sneered. 'If they could see it now— full of scrounging Wogs!—They'd turn in their graves they would—poor souls!'

Melanie allowed herself a tight-lipped smile. *Get her back on track,* she thought. 'Will you tell me more about Doctor Weldon, Vera?'

Vera's mood quickly brightened. 'Yes—sorry…For the next few weeks I really didn't see a lot of him to be honest, other than the occasional walk-past on the wards; but he always acknowledged me and sometimes,' Vera paused and smiled, 'sometimes he'd give me a cheeky wink, which sent my heart-rate *soaring*, I can tell you.'

Melanie listened in silence as the old lady appeared to rejuvenate in front of her eyes.

'But the first time Tony and I had a proper conversation was in the *pub* one Saturday night. I was there with some of the other nurses, letting off some steam, singing along to the pianist and getting a bit drunk, when *he* walked in. The place was heaving and so full of smoke it was difficult to see him across the room. We all watched excitedly as he bought himself a pint at the bar and then, to our complete surprise, he walked over to our table and asked if he could join us. It might sound silly to you but in them days us nurses were the scrapings of the social barrel and yet he chose to come and sit with us.'

Vera closed her eyes briefly and said:

'I can still remember the intoxicating smell of his aftershave. He was a charmer all right, a real ladies man—but he was bloody good company. He made us all laugh that night with his naughty jokes and innuendos. He had us all blushing he did. He kept glancing at me and I dared to think that he might fancy me. I was just sitting there, open-mouthed, spell-bound in his company, listening to his soft, lilting voice. The other nurses teased me about it for weeks afterwards. He bought all of us a drink and insisted on being introduced to each of us, in turn. I was feeling a bit tipsy at the time, which gave me the Dutch courage to introduce myself. He shook my hand, looked into my eyes, and said that it was a real pleasure to meet me…I can remember Patti getting so embarrassed when it was her turn to introduce herself she just froze like a wax model from Madam Tussauds. It made us all roar with laughter.' Vera chuckled. 'It was left to me to tell Tony her name in the end.'

Vera's expression beamed as she relived the moment.

She continued:

'He could have had any one of us that night and he knew it…but he didn't. He left us shortly afterwards and, as you can imagine, he was the topic of conversation for the rest of the evening. I remember laughing so much I wet my knickers. When I went to bed that night I fantasized about him and wanked myself to sleep.'

Shocked, Melanie raised her hand to her mouth and lowered her head to hide her blushing smile.

'What's the matter with you?… Surely you don't think you're the first generation to discover the pleasures of masturbation do you?' Vera laughed and then croaked to clear her wheezing chest before continuing:

'And then one day in April 1952, I was passing through the east-wing when he walked up to me in his white coat and asked me what I was doing on Saturday — Just like that. I was shocked to be honest, so I told him I had nothing planned…which was the truth. Then he asked me to go dancing with him. I couldn't believe it, but I eventually composed myself and accepted his invitation. That was the start of our relationship.' Vera smiled affectionately and the skin on her nose crinkled.

'He *snagged* my new stockings with his watch that first night, but I forgave him because he made me feel like a *princess.'*

Melanie smiled, warmly.

Vera then began to speak quietly. 'I eventually lost my virginity to him—on the back seat of his posh car. I never realised that kind of tenderness was possible between two people. After that I wanted him all the time. He often said to me I was sex mad! And looking back, I probably was!' Vera said, tittering. 'I can still remember the ripples of excitement that ran through my whole body when I thought about him. Wanting to be with him all the time; running my fingers through his hair and feeling him—hard as *rock*, inside me. We had a tender, sweet love that I could *never* have imagined possible; he showed me kindness and respect and he never *ever* wanted to hurt me.'

Somebody did, Melanie thought.

Vera, turned to Melanie, wiping a tear from her cheek, and said:

'I really don't think I could have been any happier… and then in an instant—like a bubble bursting—he was gone—the man I loved with all of my heart—was gone.'

Melanie had listened in silence to the old lady as she relived her memories; talking with such fondness and affection about her lover. The man she'd supposedly killed with a kitchen knife through his heart.

Melanie poised herself and asked:

'…Do *you* know who killed Doctor Weldon, Vera?'

Vera nodded. '…Someone with a motive, my dear,' she responded, tearfully.

Chapter 4

The kind of happiness that hurts

'You know the kind of happiness that hurts?' Vera gesticulated to her breast and laughed.

Melanie smiled at Vera's comment.

'…Although you might be too young to know what I'm talking about,' she added, before opening her bag and taking out a packet of Benson & Hedges and a lighter. 'Want one, my love?'

Melanie crinkled her nose and shook her head.

'No,…I didn't think so,' Vera said, before lighting up and filling her lungs with smoke.

'…Tony was such a charmer. All the girls wanted to be seen with him.' As she spoke, smoke exuded from her nose and mouth. 'But *I* was the only one he wanted.' Vera smiled and her eyes became focused on some distant object; an old memory had revisited her with such crystal clarity she could feel his warm lips on hers and hear the pulsing passion of his staccato breath as his probing hand reached her stocking tops.

Vera sighed. 'You see, I was lucky enough to be brought up in a *loving* family, but my father was killed in the war so my mother brought all seven of us up on her own. God knows how, but she did. I always remember her saying to me, Vera if you really want to be a nurse badly enough, then you will, my girl; and I did, I really wanted to be a nurse from a really young age. I don't know why because nurses weren't respected then, not like they are today.'

'Where did you grow up, Vera?' Melanie asked.

'Canterbury, my dear,' she replied.

'And so you became a nurse?'

'Yes, I did. My mother was right, wasn't she?'

Melanie nodded in agreement.

'Are any of your siblings still alive?'

'No—sadly I'm the last of them,' she said, pulling on her cigarette.

'…Please continue, Vera.'

'Yes,…sorry… Tony was a *really* good doctor. The war in North Africa had hardened him though. He told me some of the things he'd seen and done. It was terrible. Young men mutilated and driven mad by the horrors of war. That's what interested him, you know, mental illness. He told me that he was going to become a psychiatrist one day. We had quite a few mental cases at Llanarth and Tony took it on himself to care for them. Some of them were quite violent individuals and needed regular sedating to stop them killing themselves, or killing us; and not just *men*, women *too*. Most of them were harmless enough though, just mad as *a box of frogs.*'

Melanie smiled, 'Mad as a box of frogs?'

'Yeah, you know, *Doolally tap*,' Vera explained, crossing her eyes and laughing.

Melanie felt her mobile phone vibrate in her jacket pocket and while Vera was bent over, stubbing out her cigarette with her shoe, she took the chance to glance at the display. It was a text from her boss, Alan Cornish, asking:

How's it going?

Melanie quickly returned the phone to her pocket.

Alan Cornish was ex Metropolitan police and at the age of forty-seven now ran the highly successful Criminal Investigation Bureau called *Probe.* The organisation consisted of eight internal staff and three field agents, one of which was Melanie Underwood. Much of the work *Probe* acquired was from the police, desperate for additional help and expertise in solving complex crimes. The Bureau's strength and success rested on the way it cross-fertilised disciplines such as forensics, psychology, psychiatry computing, IT and good old-fashioned criminology.

Alan Cornish had met Melanie at a charity event in Cambridge and was immediately enraptured with her beauty and intellect. Having just received a first-class honours degree in psychology she was exactly what Cornish was looking for to boost his team of investigators and, on impulse, he'd offered her a job that very evening. Melanie had taken his business card and a week later she'd called him.

As soon as she was on board with *Probe,* Cornish had begun to encourage her to take an interest in *criminal* psychology and now, three-years-later, as he'd promised, he was sponsoring her part-time studies for a DPhil doctorate in the subject.

Vera raised her hand to her mouth and coughed to clear her throat… 'You wouldn't believe the series of events that led up to Tony's demise,' she said.

'Try me,' Melanie responded, flipping open her notepad and pulling a pen out of her hair.

Chapter 5

A boy or a girl?

Six years before the murder of Dr. Weldon

(East-London docklands, 1946)

The aftermath of another world war had poured more hardship on the working classes and the scars from the devastating conflict engulfed the ruined capital. The dogged remains of burnt out buildings balanced precariously on fields of rubble. And for many of the city's young children, returning from the safety of the lush countryside playground, they found a new and more exciting playground in the incongruous rat-infested piles of rubble and broken glass.

Large families of eight or more children, living in cramped conditions, were commonplace and child mortality was inevitably high. Most people in the docklands now lived in abject poverty. Some houses had the luxury of running *cold* water and a lavatory, often in outhouses and often communal.

Those shops that had escaped the relentless German bombing raids—and some that didn't—were open for business, but essentials like bread, butter and milk were scarce and the food available was limited and rationed.

In the sitting room of a dimly lit terraced house in London's docklands a coal fire blazed in the hearth. The heat it gave off was welcoming on the young girl's naked back, even though the water in the zinc bath had gone cold and a carbolic scum from the previous occupants clung to the waterline. Her legs were covered in goosebumps and a shiver shook her entire body.

The man's penetrating gaze never left her and his face donned the familiar smirk—the one she'd come to dread. In his hand he held the threadbare bath towel that she desperately longed for.

Suddenly, from upstairs, came the cry of a new-born baby.

'The baby!' she called out 'Muvver's 'ad the—'

'Don't worry yer little self 'bout that, dimwit,' he said, sneering.

'But yer needs to go and see 'er,' she said, pleadingly. 'You gotta make sure she's orite.'

'Plenyur time for that, my girl. Now get out of that tub and let me dry yer off.'

'But—the *baby*!'

'*Fuck the baby*! Come 'ere—*Now!'*

Reluctantly, the young girl stood up, cowering like a scolded dog; her nakedness glistened in the soft glow of the wall-mounted gas lamps.

'Cum to Daddy,' he said, through tight lips; his breath quickening.

'Please don't—not again,' the girl begged as she stepped out of the tub.

'Shut yer feckin mouf yer dirty little 'ore, you luvs it, I knows yer do.'

The young girl's body shook uncontrollably as the man pulled up his trousers and buttoned up his flies.

'Fore you gets dressed make up that fire, 'ear me? I needs some shut-eye 'fore I goes to work I do. And remember, if yer knows what's good for yer girl you'll keep that pretty little mouf of yers shut, or I'll slit yer feckin froat wide open…Understand me?'

As the young girl lowered her head in silent submission he settled into the armchair, closed his eyes and let out a contented sigh.

Quickly, the girl grabbed the towel off the floor and wrapped it around her trembling body. She found the feel of it comforting, like a friendly, caring arm, there to protect her from him; but she knew it was too late for that.

Upstairs the new-born had stopped crying and the living room had become eerily quiet except for the gentle hiss of the gas lamps; very soon though that was replaced by the sound of loud snoring.

The girl dressed as quickly and quietly as possible and slipped her feet into her half-brother's size eight boots.

Do it, Jessica, do it now, she urged herself.

The girl grabbed the poker off the stand in the hearth and pushed the end into the flaming coals; waiting anxiously in silence until the end was red hot. After a minute or so in the fire the glowing end started to spit little sparks that reminded her of a bonfire night sparkler.

When she finally pulled the red-hot poker out of the flames she could feel its radiant heat on her angry face. Quietly she approached him; the man who had the bloody nerve to call himself, *Daddy*! The filthy, dirty pervert who took pleasure in abusing and hurting her. Now she was close enough to touch him and smell his vile breath. Her heart was bounding in her chest, but when he snorted and shifted in his seat her heart almost stopped.

Do it—Jess—do it!

Through gritted teeth, she took a deep breath and then with both hands she lunged the poker into her stepfather's left eye. His body went rigid and his arms stiffened and convulsed as if he was sitting in the electric chair the moment the executioner closed the switch. There was a pungent smell of burning flesh as the girl, eyes wide with rage, gyrated the poker, pushing it deep into his head; searing his brains.

'You'll never do that again, will you?' she yelled, and yanked the poker with both hands, jerking the man's head from side to side. 'Good,' she said, pulling the poker out of his blackened eye socket and replacing it on its stand in the hearth.

The man's head slumped forwards and his bottom jaw hung loose. Blood trickled out of his ears and nostrils and his hands twitched for a few moments as his bladder emptied warm, acrid piss into his trousers and the cushion of the armchair.

The young girl lifted the dead man's head. 'Yer right, you'll never do that again,' she said, and spat on his face. She then walked out of the front door into Mellish Street.

She leaned over the gutter and her hungry stomach retched bile into her throat and mouth that burned hotter than the fire in the hearth.

Dressed only in her shabby cotton frock and clodhopper boots, fourteen-year-old Jessica Whatley forced her aching body down the street. She had no money and nowhere to go but she knew one thing for sure—there was no way she could go back. As she walked, she pondered. *I wonder if it was a boy or a girl? It'll be dark soon.*

The young girl felt no regrets; just pure exhilaration as adrenalin surged through her veins.

Chapter 6

A born survivor

(East London docklands 1946)

London's docklands were a hive of activity
as the wharfs began to return to full capacity now that
the war was over. With unloading done mostly
manually the place was awash with men and, without
doubt, it was a dangerous place to be, at any time,
especially for a fourteen-year-old girl.

Jessica was cold and hungry after sleeping rough for
three nights. But she was tough and very quickly she'd
found a warehouse, near the river, piled high with
wooden crates and with some old straw she'd made a
makeshift nest in the relative safety of the high, hidden
perch. She'd stolen an apple and a pork pie from a stall
in the market, together with a wooden-handled steak
knife off the table of a drunken labourer, outside one of
the many pubs opening up in the area; and that was the

39

only food she'd eaten since leaving home. Her body still ached and the bruises on her thighs were now turning from a dark-purple to a dark-yellow ochre.

At first light the chattering sound of the wharf's labour force arriving for another busy day awakened Jessica from an uneasy sleep. *He* had been there in her dreams again, he was always there, taunting her and threatening to kill her if she ever told anyone about what he did to her. She heard his rasping voice in her head:

I'll slit yer feckin froat, yer little whore, hear me? I means it I do, I'll slit yer feckin froat wide open—and that's a promise.

'Not any more you won't,' she said to herself.

She rubbed her eyes and gazed out from her makeshift bed like a lookout in a sailing ship's crow's nest. Outside, the sun was rising and beams of orange light flooded the warehouse like Super Troupers.

Hunger pains reminded her that she needed to eat and the smell of baking bread wafting through the building from a nearby bakery was like a knife in her stomach. The young girl tried not to think about her dire situation; she had no tears left to cry and she needed food.

Jessica carefully climbed down from her perch and walked out into the misty morning sunshine. A massive merchant ship was entering the Millwall dock, selfishly blocking out the sun. The air, in the shade, had a cold bite to it. Labourers loitered along the wharf smoking and chatting in small groups; waiting for the order to unload the ship's cargo of sugar and grain from the USA.

Jessica moved swiftly and stealthily out of the bustling docks area, aware that the police were probably looking for her. She headed north to Poplar and Chrisp Street Market in the hope of finding some food, or stealing it, if necessary.

When she arrived, the place was buzzing with bargain hunting women and annoyingly boisterous children flitting everywhere. An altercation had started at a nearby bread stall and a woman lay unconscious on the floor after being punched in the face by a surly looking one-toothed woman; and all over a loaf of bread!

Opposite the bread stall was a stall selling pies and Jessica walked past to assess the situation. *Could she grab one?*

There was only one person working the stall, an old lady with rosy cheeks, and she was busy attending to the woman poleaxed on the floor. Jessica made her move.

Quickly walking away she turned left into the next row of stalls and then she started to run to the east-end of the market. She devoured the pie like a hungry dog, licking her dirty fingers clean.

Next to her, a well-to-do woman was pushed to the ground by a scruffy looking youth who ran off with her bag. The woman, clearly shaken and in pain picked herself up off the floor and gazed down at her bloodied knees poking out through the holes in her stockings.

Jessica ran after the robber as he legged it down Kerbey Street. She watched him as he slipped into a narrow ally and she followed him in. As he was opening the stolen bag Jessica approached him.

'Fuck off,' he said, angrily, struggling to get his breath.

'That's not yours,' she said, pointing a finger.

'So what yer gonna do 'bout it, bitch?' he said, and made the fatal mistake of grabbing her crotch and pulling her towards him. 'How's about you sucking my —'

The knife blade entering his throat silenced him.

Jessica cringed. 'Your breath *stinks* like a sewer,' she said, and deftly twisted the wooden-handled knife deep into the side of his neck.

The youth gasped and uttered a pathetic whine before sliding down the wall; bright red blood dribbled from his mouth and down his chin. He stared up at the young girl standing over him, smiling, like a prized gladiator. With an expression of disbelief he raised a trembling hand and touched the knife handle sticking out of his neck—then, his arm dropped limply to his side.

'That's what I'm gonna do 'bout it,' she said, mockingly and wrenched the bag's strap out of his clenched fist.

Jessica walked back to the market and looked around trying to find the woman. She found her talking to a policeman and decided to bide her time, watching from a distance as the officer scribbled some notes into a little leather book while the woman blew her nose into a white linen handkerchief. A few minutes later the policeman walked off, pushing his notebook into his top pocket. Once he was out of sight Jessica approached the woman.

'I got it back for yer,' she said, holding out the bag.

The woman raised her hands to her face in sheer delight. 'Oh my *dear* girl, thank you, thank you *so* much.' She took the bag and inspected its contents. 'Everything's here! *Oh*, I am so grateful to you,' she said and opened her purse. 'Here… have this.'

Jessica held out her hand and the woman placed two crown coins on her grubby palm.

'I hope ten shillings is enough for your troubles?'

'Ta, missus,' Jessica said, having never seen so much money in her life. *That's one hundred and twenty pennies!*

'Where did you find it?' the woman asked.

Jessica scrunched up her nose. 'I knows him—he's a bit simple.'

'What?—And *little* you chastised him?' the woman said, incredulously, and giggled.

'Yeah!—He got it in the neck from me, missus.'

'What is your name, my dear?'

'People call me Curly, ma'am.' Jessica walked away clenching the coins and with three things on her mind: a bath, some new clothes and some daisy roots that actually fitted her; smugly knowing she could afford them all.

On her way out of the market, heading for Poplar Baths, she stopped at the pie stall and bought two meat pies; deliberately leaving one of them on the stall.

Where did I get the name Curly from? She wondered.

Chapter 7

You don't have a motive, do you?

'Well,' said Vera, 'I was so much in love with Tony he could have pulled my eyes out and I would have forgiven him. But after a while *he* seemed to change, he became…*indifferent,* I suppose, after the initial excitement had worn off… We were like Plutarch's Antony and Cleopatra.'

Melanie raised her eyes in surprise at the unexpected comparison.

'Not much else to do with my time, I'm afraid,' Vera explained flatly, before taking out another cigarette and lighting up.

'He became very friendly with a young psychologist called Phillip Manson and he seemed happier in his company than in mine. I'm not saying he was gay or anything like that but the two of them were always laughing and going down the pub together for a few beers, without me. I began to feel like I was an intruder. He still wanted sex with me of course, but only when it suited him.—Typical man,' she added. 'I put up with it because I loved him so much. He was the only man I've ever known to show me respect. He made me feel like I was special.'

'That's nice,' interjected Melanie.

'Yes,'…Vera said, thoughtfully. 'And then he was killed.'

So you didn't kill him, thought Melanie.

'The only man I ever loved. How cruel is that?' Tears poured down her cheeks as Vera looked at Melanie, leaving little lines in her powder puff makeup.

'So who was it that killed him, Vera?'

Vera stared straight ahead for a long time. 'I remember it like it was yesterday. It was six o'clock in the evening when I walked from the nurse's block down to Tony's office, because he'd said to me earlier, in the canteen, that he *wanted* me on his desk, that night. I remember how moist I was as I walked there, knowing what to expect. He was a *bloody* good lover,' Vera added. 'I remember checking my seams before I knocked on his door, but there was no answer so I opened it and walked in. Tony was slumped on his desk. There was blood everywhere. When I got close to him I noticed a carving knife in his back. That's when everything went black and I passed out.'

'So you didn't see who killed him?'

'No, I didn't.'

'Do you have any idea who could have done such a thing, Vera? Did someone have a grudge against him, for instance?'

Vera wiped her tears away with a tissue and inhaled deeply. 'I have my suspicions,' she said, quietly.

'Will you tell me?'

'…I can think of *three* people who *might've* wanted Tony dead.' Vera raised her finger. 'You must remember, we were a *secur*e institution with a lot of drugs on the premises, hard drugs, opiates, you know the sort. I'd had my suspicions for some time that a nurse named Sally Griffith was involved with a local gang and she was taking drugs off the premises on a regular basis. I told Tony about it and he said he was going to keep a close watch on her.'

'And you think this, Sally Griffith, killed Doctor Weldon because he found out she was stealing them?'

'I don't know; maybe not her.—These gangs were *ruthless*; not the sort to mess with.'

'So who are your other suspects, Vera?'

'There was a patient named… Doris, she's dead now, overdosed, she was a real nutcase. Fancied Tony something rotten. Always asking him to fuck her she was. And then one day she flipped, shouting and screaming that she was going to kill him. The morning after Tony had been murdered it was reported that Doris's door had been unlocked all night and nobody had an explanation for why it had happened. How bloody strange is that?'

Melanie continued to take notes as Vera talked.

'And your third suspect, Vera?' she asked.

'…One evening, I arrived at Tony's office. The door was ajar and just before I knocked I heard Phillip Manson saying in a very serious tone: *If this gets out, Tony, I will kill you, and that's a promise.* When I knocked I was told to wait before I was allowed to enter. I remember how sheepish they both looked when I eventually walked in.'

'So you went into detention for a murder *you* didn't commit. Why?'

Vera took a deep breath. '…I'd lost the *only* person in the world who truly cared about me. The one I loved with such passion it hurt. My head seemed to explode. Nothing mattered any more, there was no reason to carry on. I couldn't think or speak. My brain simply shut down like a computer.'

'A natural defence against *severe* trauma, Vera; the brain's very own safety mechanism,' Melanie explained.

Vera nodded gently and smiled.

Melanie noticed the old lady was suddenly looking drawn; revisiting the past had taken its toll on her, draining her of precious energy.

Eventually Vera said, meekly:

'I'm sorry to waste your time, Melanie,'

'It *wasn't* a waste of time, Vera.'

'Well, you came to find out *my* motive for killing Tony and you *still* don't have a motive, do you?'

'It's better than that, I have *three*, Vera?'

Vera chuckled. 'Yes, but *which* motive is the *real* motive for murder?'

Melanie closed her note book and said, thoughtfully:

'At this moment in time, Vera, I have no idea.'

But I do intend to find out.

When Melanie returned to her car she slumped into the driver's seat. She felt emotionally exhausted from her meeting with Vera and exhaled loudly before glancing into the driver's mirror. 'Oh Christ! You look like shit!' she said.

Melanie closed her eyes in pensive mood.

Somebody out there has got away with murder because it wasn't Vera Parsons who killed him; I'm convinced of that, Alan Cornish.

Chapter 8

My money's on Manson

When Melanie Underwood walked into the building, her boss, Alan Cornish, called her into his office. He was sitting at his desk and he gestured to Melanie to sit on a conference chair he'd pulled up in anticipation.

'Well,' he said, 'how did you get on?'

Melanie smiled. 'That was a *very* interesting meeting.'

'Did she tell you her *motive* for killing…what's his name?' He leaned forward to read his notes… 'Doctor Anthony Weldon?'

'I don't think Vera Parsons killed him.'

'What?'

'She loved him and spent years in a secure mental hospital—but I'm convinced she didn't killed him. Let's not forget that after Weldon's murder she was considered *unfit* to plead before the trial and was *never* actually charged with his murder, instead she was committed to a secure institution. When she eventually began to communicate again she was assessed and released without ever having a criminal record.'

'So she got away with murder then?'

Melanie shook her head in frustration.

'So if it wasn't her then who did it?'

'That's what I asked her but she said she didn't know, and I believe her, Alan.'

Cornish glanced at his notes again. 'Why did she stop talking for all those years?'

Melanie sighed. 'She said it felt like her head had exploded when she found Weldon's body. As if her brain had switched off just like a computer. Weldon seems to be the first person she ever had a loving relationship with. *He* was someone she trusted.'

'Do you believe her?'

'…She seems genuine enough, Alan. I must admit she had the *means* and the *opportunity* to kill him but right now there doesn't seem to be a *motive* for killing him.'

'They were lovers…Romeo and Juliet, Samson and Delilah, Antony and Cleopatra.'

'Yeah…yeah, Miss Piggy and Kermit the frog!'

'There's your motive!' Cornish chuckled.

Melanie raised her hands in a gesture of acceptance. 'Alan, I know exactly what you mean. But I don't think it was like that with them. I *really* think somebody else killed Doctor Weldon.'

Cornish tapped his finger tips together as he looked into Melanie's almond-shaped eyes. 'Coffee?'

'Can I have a tea please?' Melanie asked.

Alan Cornish walked out of the office to the kitchenette and returned with a coffee and a tea on a plastic tray.

Melanie thought how smart he looked in his dark suit, white shirt and red tie. He offered Melanie her tea and then he returned to his chair.

He was six-feet-two and in good shape for his forty-seven years. His once raven-black hair was now peppered with grey around his temples but his mysterious dark eyes were still sharp and bright and his chiseled features undermined his age.

It intrigued Melanie why he'd never got married. She wasn't even sure if he had a partner. He certainly never talked about one. When she thought about it she knew very little about her boss outside of their professional relationship.

It would be such a waste if he was gay, she thought.

For a while they sipped their drinks in silence.

'I'm sorry you didn't get your motive,' he finally said.

'Actually, I got *three*.'

Cornish frowned. 'How come?'

'Vera Parsons gave me *three* names of people she thought had reasons to kill her lover.'

'Go on,' Cornish said, leaning forward.

'The first was a nurse,' Melanie opened her notebook, 'by the name of Sally Griffith. Vera reckons she was stealing drugs from the hospital to supply a local gang.'

'And Weldon found out?'

'We don't know for sure. It's just Vera's supposition.'

Cornish nodded, thoughtfully. 'She would have had the means and the opportunity.'

'Yeah, she would have. Then there was a patient that Vera called Doris. It sounds like she was a right nutcase. Died from an overdose, according to Vera. Apparently this Doris woman made it quite clear that she was going to kill Doctor Weldon. Strangely, the morning after Weldon's murder her cell door was reported to have been unlocked!'

'Opportunity and means… but where's the motive? Christ ! This is turning into an Agatha Christie whodunnit!'

Melanie nodded, wide-eyed. 'And the third and final suspect is our junior clinical psychologist, Phillip Manson, work colleague and drinking partner of Doctor Weldon. Vera reckons she overheard him in Weldon's office saying.'—Melanie checked her notes again and quoted:

'*If this gets out I will kill you, Tony, and that's a promise.*'

'Opportunity, means and *motive!* My money's on Manson,' Cornish said, jovially. 'But, *unfortunately* we'll never know.'

'Oh, please don't say that Alan!'

'Hey! Come on!—We don't have the time to investigate this on—you *know* that. All we can do is tell the police what she told you; but I don't honestly think for one moment they'll pick up on it. After all it's simply an old woman's suspicions. Nothing more than that!'

'Someone has got away with *murder*, Alan.'

'You're right—but that's not *our* problem at the moment, Melanie. We have far more important cases that we're actually getting paid *handsomely* to investigate. So please, get back to what's important for Probe.'

'But think of the *prestige* we'd get if we solved this intriguing murder,' Melanie argued.

Cornish looked into Melanie's puppy-dog eyes.

'…The answer is *no*,' he said, defiantly.

Melanie lowered her head, knowing Alan wasn't going to change his mind.

'Come on,' he said, with an air of sympathy, 'back to work.'

'Okay,' Melanie muttered and stood up. 'But you can't blame me for trying,' she added, and walked out of the office closing the door behind her.

'I don't blame you, I admire your enquiring mind, young lady,' he said, quietly.

It was one of the reasons why he employed her.

Cornish looked down at Melanie's steaming cup of tea on the edge of his desk before turning his attention to Vera Parsons's case file; *just* while he finished his coffee.

Melanie sat down at her desk having said hello to the other staff in the office and glanced at the wall clock. It was 15.30. *Today's gone quickly,* she thought, settling into her chair and switching on her iMac to read her emails. At 16.00 Alan Cornish walked over to her desk. She looked up at him and smiled.

'Have you got a minute?' he asked.

'Sure,' she responded.

'Good; come back to my office when you're ready.'

'What's up?' she asked, tentatively.

'It's about Vera,' he said.

'What about her?'

'Bring a fresh tea with you, your other one went cold, and a latte for me, please… Are you in a hurry to get away tonight?'

'…No, why?'

'Good,' he replied, before turning and heading back to his office.

Melanie walked to kitchenette; her spirits lifted, but somewhat confused by her boss's apparent change of mind.

What the hell has grabbed his attention now? She pondered.

Chapter 9

I don't want to go to hell

(Putney, London 1947)

Porky was the first person Jessica ever trusted. They met some eleven month's ago, when she was buying food at his dad's grocery stall in the market near the guest house where she now worked, and they had become instant friends.

He was as thin-as-a-rake, gangly and alway cheerful; even when there was nothing to be cheerful about. His hair was shaved at the sides leaving a curly ginger mop on the top of his head. Both his front teeth were missing after he'd ridden his bicycle into a hole in the road and he talked with a slight lisp. He was Jessica's best friend, and she was his.

After leaving the docklands, Jessica, with the little money she had, took lodgings and quickly found that the lady owner, Mrs Oliver, was desperate for help with the demands of the growing number of workers coming to town needing somewhere to sleep. Jessica took the job, working for a pittance changing beds, cleaning, washing, ironing, cooking and shopping, but at least she had a bed of her own in a tiny little attic room and food to eat—every day. But most of all she was free of the monster who'd abused her, hurt her and made her cry every day of her young life. At night in her little bed she would sob incessantly, yearning for someone to hold her and comfort her, knowing in her broken heart that it would never really happen. Eventually exhaustion would take over her tired body and sleep would bring her some peace of mind for a few precious hours.

In the afternoons, when she was busy in the kitchen, Porky would often call by and she would pour him a glass of milk and let him choose a biscuit out of the cork-topped jar.

One particular Sunday afternoon, Porky called by and Jessica sensed he was not his normal jovial self.

'What's the matter with yer then?'

'Nuffink's the matter with me! Gotta a biscuit for me 'ave yer, Jess?'

'There is, Porky,' she said, ignoring his request. 'What's the matter? If you don't tell me yer won't get a biscuit.'

Porky looked up at the glass jar, longingly. '…I can't say, Jess. If I tells yer I'll go to Hell.'

'Who told yer that then?' she asked.

Porky lowered his head in silence. Jessica grabbed the biscuit jar and waved it in front of her friend. 'Who told you that?'

'I *don't* wanna go to Hell, Jess.'

'Yer won't go to Hell, stupid. Hell is for *bad* people, not people like you Porky; yer okay.'

Porky smiled. 'I ent a bad person, am I, Jess?'

'No, you ent; so what's bothering you?' Jessica opened the lid and the smell of sweet ginger wafted out.

Porky swallowed hard, staring at the jar.

'Tell me,' she said, demandingly.

'If I tells yer will yer *promise* not to a say a word to *anyone?*'

'I promise.'

Porky looked into her bright, expectant eyes. She was his best friend and he believed her. He knew she really did care about him.

'…You knows I go to church, singing in the choir and all that.'

'Yeah, I knows that.'

'Well…'

'…Well what, Porky?'

'…I don't know how's to say it to yer Jess.'

Suddenly, Jessica went cold, raising her hands to her face '…Have yer gone and got molested, Porky?'

'Whah?' He said with a confused stare.

'Yer knows what I mean. As someone bin messing with yer?—Touching yer *privates*?' she asked, gesticulating with her hand.

Porky sighed. '…Yeah,' he said, and wiped his wet eyes with the back of his hand. 'I knows it ent right… but *he* said I'd go to hell if I didn't do it; and now it's happening again.'

'This, *He*, Porky—is it Father Thomas?'

Porky lowered is head in shame and nodded. Jessica handed him the open jar and he took the biggest biscuit he could find.

The evening service had finished some thirty minutes earlier when Jessica arrived at the church. She noticed the vestry light was still on as she pushed the heavy main door open. Inside the tranquil church the air was cool and heavy with the sweet scent of incense. As she walked down the nave towards the altar she looked up to see a mournful looking figure of Christ peering down at her from the cross. A crown of thorns punctured his bloodied head. She gazed at the gaping wounds to his near naked body and the large nails that were driven through his hands and feet. It was the image of suffering, a broken man near to death, and she could almost feel his pain. *So cruel,* she thought, as she turned left at the altar towards the strip of light shining from under the vestry door.

When she neared the door it opened and a young chorister dressed in a red cassock and white tunic faced her with his head lowered.

'Get changed and go home, boy. And remember, say *nothing!*' came a forceful voice from within the vestry.

'Yes, Father,' replied the young boy before walking past Jessica without looking up.

Jessica knocked on the open door.

'What is it now?'

She entered the room and stood looking at the old priest sitting at his desk.

'Oh! I do apologise. I thought you were someone else,' he said.

'Father Thomas?'

'That's me—for my sins,' he said, jovially.

'I'm a friend of Porky, he sings in your choir.'

'Porky?…Oh yes… we know him as Raymond, Raymond Bannister; a bit on the thin side but never-the-less a lovely lad. And so you want to join our little band of choristers do you, young lady? Well, you'd better come in then. Please close the door behind you.'

Jessica could imagine him doing those disgusting things to her best friend; things Porky finally admitted to after his second biscuit. She watched as the priest eyed her with a smirk on his face that made her visibly shiver.

'Oh my dear, you're cold,' the priest said, sounding concerned. 'Come and sit next to me by the fire young lady and tell me your name and a little bit about yourself.'

Jessica sat down opposite the priest next to the blazing fire that illuminated his ruddy, bearded face and glistening, moist forehead.

'The fire will warm you up in no time.' He placed his hands on her knees. 'Now tell me, what is your name?'

'Jessica,' she said, looking down at his trembling hands.

'And you've come here to join our choir, Jessica?'

'No,… that's not why I'm here.'

'Oh! …I assumed you wanted to join Raymond in the choir.'

'No, not at all, Father.'

'So why have you come here tonight?' he asked, as he slid his hand up the inside of her thigh.

'I've come here to *kill* you!' she said, coldly.

Startled, Father Thomas pulled back and Jessica smiled. A moment later the priest started laughing. He looked up, as if he was about to speak to God in the Heavens. Still laughing, he uttered his last words: 'She's come here to—'

That's when Jessica pulled the kitchen knife from her coat and stabbed him in the neck.

Father Thomas's head slumped backwards in the chair and with his eyes wide open he coughed a fountain of blood that coated his face like a red mask.

Jessica then pulled the long knife blade out of his neck and drove it deep into his chest. Adrenalin surged through her veins as she pulled the knife out and wiped the blade clean in the priest's cassock. Then she grabbed him under his arms and pulled his limp body out of the seat. Gently, she lowered his frail frame onto his knees facing the blazing hearth and with a gentle push she watched as he toppled into the roaring flames. His head landed in the heart of the fire and immediately his white hair and beard ignited, burning off like fire crackers. His facial skin started to blister and pop like a pig on a spit, quickly turning black as bright orange flames engulfed his head.

It's a shame he's dead, she thought. *Cos that would be very painful.*

Jessica then picked up the poker from its holder in the inglenook fireplace and leaned over the priest's body. She forced the pointed end deep into the back of his blistering neck. Using the poker as a lever she heaved his torso into the roaring flames before standing back, hot and breathless, as the priest's cassock began to burn.

Father Thomas's clothes and meagre body fat were quite sufficient to fuel the fire. Outside, thick black smoke ascended from the vestry's chimney into the equally black night sky, only to be caught up in the descending smog that would be particularly *acrid* around the Putney area tonight.

Moments later Jessica walked back through the nave. She stopped and turned to look at the crucifix. 'You understand, don't you?' she said, and smiled.—'I *knew* you would,' she said, and promptly walked out, closing the main door behind her. She traipsed, trance like, down the path to the lych-gate; adrenalin still surging through her veins. As she closed the gate, Father Thomas's head burst open in the hearth.

He worked for the Devil, she thought, as she walked back, in the shadows, towards her tiny bedsit. In her mind's eye she could see Porky's toothless grin; happy in the knowledge that Father Thomas was no longer going to abuse him.

There's too many evil people—and if they tries to 'urt me—or my friends, I'll kill 'em.—I like it,—I likes the feeling I gets knowing that I've removed 'em from this world — never to do again what they lusts for.—I kills monsters—that's what I do—and I like it, she mused, as her B&B came into view. *I just wish I could kill the ghost that visits me in the night, then I'd be 'appy again.* 'But you can't kill ghosts, Jessica, because they're already dead,' she reminded herself.

Jessica unlocked the kitchen door of the B&B and walked into the darkness. She washed the knife in the sink with cold water and soap and wiped it clean before hanging it up on the rack above the preparation table. She then quietly made her way up the four flights of stairs to her attic room. Once inside her tiny room she locked the door and undressed, then she slipped into her cotton nightgown and crawled into bed. For a long time she waited under the sheets for *Him* to come and taunt her with his threats and vile breath, but thankfully he didn't come, and as a police car pulled up at the church, Jessica fell into a deep, undisturbed sleep.

When the dawn finally arrived the sun failed to break through the thick ochre smog that hung over Putney like a rancid blanket. It seemed that even in death Father Thomas was able to inflict misery on the people of his parish.

Chapter 10

She is the only one still alive

Alan Cornish noticed Melanie arriving with the tray of drinks and opened the office door for her.

'Thank you,' she said, and walked in.

One of her colleagues at *Probe,* Olly Mathias, was sitting in front of Alan's desk. Olly was about the same age as Alan Cornish but his head was shaven and he donned a long grey Hell's-Angels-like beard. Not surprisingly his office nickname was Zeezee. Olly was an expert on relational databases and object-oriented programming, and in his twenties helped Oracle create a world beating product. Now, he was an expert on search engines and the algorithms that they use to troll the index's of the world-wide-web. But the real asset to *Probe* was Olly's experience gained at GCHQ and his knowledge of the Dark Web; the Bitcoin trading place of the criminal underworld and the secret communications platform of paedophiles and perverts.

'Hi, Melanie,' he said, as she entered.

'Zeezee, how are you?'

'Very well thank you, Melanie.'

'I didn't bring you a drink I'm sorry,' she said to Zeezee, as she handed Cornish his coffee.

'Just put one out thanks, Melanie,' he replied.

'Melanie sat down, intrigued to know what was going on.'

'Zeezee has done a bit of digging, Melanie,' Cornish explained.

'Regarding what?'

'Vera Parsons.'

Melanie frowned. 'I thought you…'

'Let me explain,' Cornish interrupted. 'I was reading her file whilst I finished my coffee and in the back of my mind I thought I'd heard the name, Phillip Manson, before. I got Zeezee to check it out for me.' Cornish gestured to Zeezee.

'Phillip Manson was *murdered* in June 1970; the police file is still open. There were no witnesses, no fingerprints and no suspects. All we know at the moment is that he wasn't a real psychologist. When he worked with Weldon he had fake qualifications.'

'Where was he killed?'

'In York; his throat was slashed and they found his genitalia in his jacket pocket. His body was found about two weeks after the murder hanging upside down from a beam with a kitchen knife protruding out of the top of his head.'

Melanie cringed. 'So what has this got to do with Vera Parsons?'

Zeezee raised a finger. 'Maybe nothing—but *she* was released in the same year that Manson was murdered, March, to be precise; having been assessed as safe to live back in the community.'

Melanie looked at Cornish, who simply raised his eyebrows. 'She had no reason to kill Manson, Alan.'

'Unless, Melanie, Manson killed her lover.'

Zeezee continued. 'Also, I found some useful information about Doris Harris.'

'She died of an overdose, according to Vera,' Melanie added.

'Not so! Doris is actually still alive.'

'What!' Melanie exclaimed.

'She was a patient at Llanarth, that's true, but she wasn't mad like they thought she was, she was suffering from a bladder infection that poisoned her blood. It was Sepsis that turned her loopy. She made a full recovery and is currently living as a widow in an old people's home in a place called Caerleon, near

Newport, in South Wales. It's an old Roman settlement and boasts a Roman baths and amphitheatre. Seems like a very nice place to visit,' Zeezee added; sounding like a tour operator.

'Could we get to see her?' Melanie asked, excitedly.

'Why?' Cornish asked.

'I'd like to ask her about Vera Parsons. Find out if she's really telling the truth.'

'Loopy Doris might not be a reliable witness?'

'She's not loopy now Alan; at least I hope she's not. It's worth a chance isn't it?' argued Melanie.

'Well, she is the *only* one still alive,' interjected Zeezee, looking at Cornish. 'Sally Griffith died of liver cancer nineteen years ago.'

Cornish smiled at Zeezee. 'Isn't Caerleon near the Celtic Manor Golf Resort where they held the 2010 Ryder Cup and where Barrack Obama stayed?'

'You *know* it is, Alan,' Zeezee said, raising his eyes.

Chapter 11

And what was her motive?

When Alan Cornish reached the M6 motorway he set the cruise control on his three-week-old Loire Blue V8 XJ Jaguar. The drive from Cambridge had been pretty steady and the traffic had been relatively light. The sat nav's designation was set to the Celtic Manor Golf Resort and their ETA of 18.00 was displayed on the screen.

'Another two hour's drive, with no hold-ups,' Cornish advised.

'When are you going to tell me the truth?' Melanie asked, inquisitively, ignoring his comment.

Cornish grinned like a child. 'What do you mean?'

'You know exactly what I mean, Alan. I don't believe we're doing this just so that you can play golf at the—what's it called?'

'The Celtic Manor.'

'Whatever…So, tell me why you changed your mind?'

Cornish glanced at Melanie and smiled. 'Just a gut feeling—no more than that—and a chance to play golf at the Celtic Manor with my *new* golf clubs,' he added with a broad grin.

Melanie gave him a gentle shove. 'Tell me what it is, this gut feeling of yours?'

'Have you ever tried to explain a gut feeling? It has no substance, nothing I can point to specifically, except perhaps the murder of Phillip Manson.'

'Do you really think Vera Parsons killed him… and I suppose by implication, Weldon too?'

'It's possible.'

'And what was her *motive*?'

'I don't know the answer to that. But I'd like to find out.'

'So, is this an *official* investigation now?' Melanie asked.

'…Let's see how I do on the golf course first.'

'Alan!'

Cornish laughed.

Melanie showed Cornish the weather app on her phone. 'Have you seen the weather forecast?'

'No—why?'

'It's going to be *very* hot tomorrow.'

Cornish glanced at the display. '*Thirty degrees*! In Wales? I don't believe it.'

'Did you bring your shorts?'

'No, I've brought a balaclava and a wet suit!' he replied.

At 18.05 Alan Cornish indicated right off the A48 dual carriageway into the Celtic Manor's main entrance. He drove over a bridge that crossed the busy M4 motorway and headed up a curving incline until an illuminated sign saying *parking spaces available* came into view. He followed the directions and parked up in the hotel's underground car park. Cornish turned off the engine and looked at Melanie. 'What time's your appointment in the morning?'

'I'm seeing Doris Harris at ten o'clock,' Melanie replied.

'Okay, take the car then, it's only ten minutes away down the hill; I won't need it.' He pressed a button. 'There you go, the sat nav is set up for you; three and a bit miles to your destination.'

'Do you trust me with your *new* car?'

'Of course. Come on let's get booked in, I'm starving!'

Melanie felt a little foolish as she walked from the lift to her hotel room. The thought that Alan might have booked a double room had been in the back of her mind.

You are stupid ! He wouldn't do such a thing as that.

Our relationship is purely professional and he is a gentleman, she mused as she swiped the card reader on the door. *So much for your fatuous thoughts my girl; our rooms are not even on the same floor for Christ's sake!*

Melanie was beautiful, but in some ways her beauty had been a hindrance to her love life. She could count the men she'd had on two fingers. Both her relationships had fallen apart because both her partners were *extremely* jealous and untrusting, which was *completely* unwarranted. Talking to other men was considered a sin and having to explain her actions, as if she'd done something wrong was—tiring. In the end she decided to go it alone.

In floods of tears, after her last relationship had broken down, she'd told her mother:

'Men are just not worth the effort.'

Her mother had wrapped her arms around her and pointed out that she was still young, very attractive and there would be plenty of time to find her Mister Right. She could hear her mother's voice saying:

You'll recognise him when you see him, my love. Just like I did with your Dad. I'll make us a lovely cup of tea—that always helps, and the thought made Melanie smile as she dropped her overnight bag on the bed and stripped naked. *It's no wonder I like tea,* she mused, as she walked into the bathroom.

'Time for a long, cool shower.'

When Melanie checked her watch it was 7.30pm. Alan had phoned earlier to say he would call for her at seven thirty. He'd told her that he'd booked a table at *Steak on Six;* knowing that Melanie loved steak.

She was inspecting her makeup in the bathroom mirror when there was a double knock on her room door.

'That will have to do,' she said, to herself, in the mirror. Melanie then opened the door to Cornish and watched as his mouth dropped open. She was wearing an above-the-knee black-silk chiffon dress from Valentino, complimented by a string of pearls around her neck. She was holding a Jimmy Choo Celeste clutch bag and wearing black high-heels from Alexander McQueen. Her shoulder-length, sun-kissed corn-coloured hair had a natural curl and her glossy lipstick matched the colour of her ruby-red nail varnish.

Cornish pointed to her pearls, praying that what he was about to say wouldn't betray what he was actually thinking. '…They're um, they're *real,* aren't they?' he managed.

'I presume you mean the pearls?' she asked, teasingly, 'yes, they are… What do you think? Do you think I'm a bit overdressed?'

'No—no—not at all…I think you look… *stunning.*'

'Thank you, Alan.'

He wanted to say so much more to her, but the words just wouldn't come; in the end he managed:

'Come on, I'm starving.'

Melanie closed her room door and asked:

'So what's this S*ex at Six* all about?'

Alan laughed, '*Steak on Six;* it comes highly recommended.'

'Does it. By whom?'

'Trip Advisor,' he said, pressing button 6 as they entered the lift. 'It's a steak restaurant on floor six.'

'Really!' Melanie exclaimed, touching his arm.

'Probably not as good as sex at six though,' Cornish added.

Melanie laughed. 'Probably not!'

The weather forecast was turning out to be accurate. When Melanie awoke at 06.45 the temperature outside was already 18 degrees. The view from her room looked over part of the Roman Road's golf course, one of three courses on the complex, and up to the golf academy and Dylan's Fitness Club.

Alan had explained over dinner to drive up to club and exit the resort from there; the sat-nav would then direct her down the hill to the nursing home in Caerleon. He'd also told her to park at the *Twenty-Ten* clubhouse when she returned from seeing Doris Harris and he would meet her there after his round of golf, hopefully between one-thirty and two. They could then discuss Melanie's findings over lunch at *Rafters*, the *Twenty-Ten* clubhouse restaurant.

Cornish had chosen to have breakfast in his bedroom after a morning swim and Melanie decided to do the same, ordering coffee, muesli and scrambled eggs with crispy bacon for 08.00; but she'd chosen a morning jog rather than a swim.

She opened the sliding doors onto the balcony and stepped outside with a cup of steaming coffee, smiling, as she thought about last night's evening meal and how much she'd enjoyed Alan's company; sharing a delicious sliced steak that was served up in a curved terracotta tile, warmed by candles underneath, and washed down with a bottle of red wine that was simply divine. At the end of the evening he'd walked her back to her room. Cornish had kissed her hand and said to her that he couldn't remember the last time that he enjoyed himself so much in such delightful company.

She remembered standing next to him outside her door wanting to kiss him on the lips; but she'd resisted the temptation. *Probably a wise decision,* she thought, but she wasn't entirely convinced.

Chapter 12

I could have killed him

At 09.35 Melanie accelerated Alan Cornish's car out of the Celtic Manor Resort and headed for Caerleon.

The weather was hotting up and she wished she'd brought something more appropriate to wear, but the grey pin-stripe suit and cream blouse would have to do. She set the Jaguar's air-con to a comfortable 20 degrees and, as directed by the lady's voice, turned right down Christchurch Hill towards her destination.

After crossing the Usk River bridge she continued through the village's one way system, past the Roman Museum and baths on her right, which Zeezee had mentioned the other day, and, as instructed, she turned right when she reached the village common, into the walled entrance of *Caerleon House*.

The sat-nav's dulcet female voice announced: 'You have reached your destination.'

Melanie checked her watch, it was 09.50.

Perfect, she thought, as she parked up and stepped out into the warm sunshine. She removed her suit jacket and laid it down on the back seat. *I won't be needing that.*

Doris Harris was your archetypal old lady, thinning permed white hair, fixed with far too much hairspray, large-framed glasses that desperately needed cleaning and pink lipstick that had found it's way to her front teeth; but her smile was intoxicating and her happy disposition was infectious.

'They said you were coming today, but I'm a bit confused about what it is you want, dear,' the old lady said in a soft voice as Melanie settled into an armchair next to her.

'I would like to ask you some questions about your time at Llanarth Court, if that's okay with you.'

'*Llanarth*! Oh my dear, that was a *such* a long time ago.'

'Yes, I know,' Melanie said, nodding. 'May I call you Doris?'

'Yes, of course, that's my name…So why would you want to ask me about Llanarth, young lady?'

'It's not so much about you Doris. I'm very interested to know more about a lady named Vera Parsons.'

'…Isn't she the woman who killed the doctor?'

'Supposedly, although she's adamant it wasn't her who killed him.'

'Well, she went to prison for it, didn't she?'

'No, she didn't actually go to prison. The case never went to court.'

'Oh, I thought she did.'

'Do you remember her, Doris?'

'Oh yes, very well; although I must say my memories of Llanarth aren't *pleasant* ones. It was an awful place to go to. I was there for about four weeks all together. They were treating me as if I was mad and looking back on it now I probably was at the time.' The old lady giggled like a young child. 'I had a kidney infection you see and it turned me daft. Eventually I got treated for it and thank God I recovered quite quickly and they sent me home.'

'Did you see much of Vera Parsons while you were there, Doris?'

'Yes, most days. I remember her well, she was quite nice to me. Not like some of the ignorant pigs that worked there!'

'Do you remember a Doctor Weldon?'

'Yes, I do, that's the man she killed, isn't it?'

'*Supposedly* killed, yes.'

'Obviously you don't think she did it; and—I must admit, young lady, I am inclined to agree with you.'

'Why is that, Doris?'

'Because Vera was head-over-heels in love with him. Her *beloved* doctor was all she ever talked about.'

'What was he like?' Melanie asked.

'Oh, he was a real ladies man. Good looking chap, he was.'

'…Is it true that you threatened to kill him?'

Doris looked shocked. '*Me*? …Why would I want to kill the him? Mind you, when I was delirious I could have said or done anything,' she stressed, and giggled again. The old lady paused and took a sip of water from a glass on the table next to her. Then she continued:

'The man I really loathed though was a chap called Phillip Manson; I *could* have killed him,' she added. Doris crinkled up her nose. 'He really was a *horrible* man.'

'Actually, somebody did kill him, years later.'

'Really! How exciting; who did it?—Who killed him, my dear?'

'We don't know. The murderer was never caught. Manson was a friend of Doctor Weldon, wasn't he?'

Doris frowned. 'Yes, that's right, he was, but I'm not sure why; they were two *very* different characters. Vera was always moaning about the fact that the pair of them were drinking too much... How did he die, my dear?' Doris asked, excitedly.

'Someone cut his throat.'

'Oh good!' Doris enthused.

Melanie decided not to mention his severed genitals and the fact that he was found hanging upside down from a beam with a kitchen knife protruding through the top of his head!

'He wasn't actually a *real* psychologist—he had fake qualifications. As a matter of fact he's a bit of an *enigma* to be honest.'

Doris nodded, knowingly. 'That explains why he was a *complete* incompetent. Nobody liked his arrogant and often rude manner, apart from the Doctor of course; which was strange in a way because they were like chalk and cheese really. Manson was nothing like Doctor Weldon; Weldon was a *good,* caring doctor.'

'Doris—are you aware of any reason why Vera Parsons might have killed Doctor Weldon?'

The old lady frowned and shook her head. '...No, not at all my dear; she seemed very happy. And, to be fair to the Doctor, I don't think there were any shenanigans going on; although *he* must have had plenty of opportunities, being surrounded by young women most of the time. The whole thing is a complete mystery to me.'

Yeah, me too, thought Melanie.

Doris Harris seemed to focus on some distant object. '…It's hard to believe but all happened such a long time ago now, my dear; I was a young woman then in the *prime* of my life,' she said, with an air of sadness in her voice.

Alan Cornish looked weary as he sipped his latte coffee beneath a large parasol outside the Celtic Manor's Twenty-Ten clubhouse. When he saw Melanie walking out of the main building towards him he smiled and waved.

'Come and join me in the shade,' he said.

Melanie looked radiant as she approached.

'How did you get on?' Cornish asked.

'Good—how about you? You look *knackered!*'

'I am knackered,' he said. 'That course is magnificent, but it's also bloody brutal. It doesn't take prisoners! And the heat didn't help. It was more like playing at midday in *Portugal!'*

'How did you get on with your *new* clubs?'

Cornish sipped his coffee. '…How do you fancy driving back to Cambridge?'

Melanie laughed. 'Yes, okay.'

Cornish waved down a waiter and ordered a pint of Moretti lager for himself and an espresso for Melanie.

'So how was Doris Harris?'

'I think Vera's innocent.'

'Really!'

Melanie settled down at the bench table opposite Cornish and looked down at the 18th green that was guarded by a large pond and water fountain. 'I bet there's some golfballs in there,' she said.

'Yes, there is,' Cornish replied, 'and one of them is mine.'

Melanie smiled, sympathetically. 'Oh dear!'

'Come on then, give us the lowdown.'

'Doris Harris basically confirmed everything that Vera told me. They were *definitely* lovers and there was no obvious friction between them. Doris said that she believed Weldon was behaving himself too, even though she described him as a ladies man. It doesn't appear to be a crime of passion that's for sure. Manson didn't score too many points with Doris though. She said he was a horrible incompetent that nobody liked, except for Weldon.'

'Do you think Weldon eventually sussed-him-out and Manson murdered him to shut him up?'

Melanie nodded. 'It's beginning to look a lot like that isn't it? It's strange though that Weldon seemed to like Manson when everyone else *detested* him.'

Cornish drained the last of his coffee and said:

'Sounds to me like Weldon was a very poor judge of character, doesn't it?'

Melanie nodded and frowned. 'Yes, it does.'

'So, Doris Harris is no longer a *suspect* then?'

'Doris had no motive to kill Weldon. I think that her threats to kill him, which was *news* to her by the way, were simply the ramblings of someone suffering from a temporary form of insanity brought on by the septicaemia.'

'Or simply Vera's *wild* imaginings!' Cornish suggested.

At that moment a waitress arrived with the cold lager and Melanie's coffee. Cornish closed his eyes and took a long swig of the Moretti.'Oh my God!—I needed that.'

'Alan, your face is looking very red.'

'I know, I forgot to wear my balaclava!'

Melanie laughed. *I like you, Alan, I like you a lot,* she thought. 'Did you play on your own?'

'No, I played in a four-ball with some of the members; a Dave, Kevin and Martin. They were all good golfers and really friendly too. I throughly enjoyed their Welsh banter, although the only one who actually spoke Welsh was Kevin; and he was a bloody *Englishman*!'

'Well, I'm glad you enjoyed it. Did you win?'

'Thanks for offering to drive back, I really appreciate it.'

Melanie laughed and sipped her coffee.

Hearing familiar voices approaching, Cornish turned around. 'Gentlemen,' he said, 'this is Melanie, my colleague. Melanie, this is Kevin David and Martin, the guys I played golf with today.'

Melanie stood up and shook hands with the three men who'd arrived on the terrace with drinks in their hands.

'We did ask him to join us,' Martin said, 'but he insisted that he had work to do.'

Cornish laughed. 'It's true, I'm afraid, and sadly we have to return to Cambridge tonight,' he answered, 'but thank you once again for the game fellas. I really enjoyed it.'

'Our pleasure,' replied Kevin, 'you played some decent golf today, Alan.'

'Thank you,' beamed Cornish, glancing at Melanie. 'This is Kevin, Melanie, the Englishman who speaks Welsh.'

'At least we think he does,' added David, dryly, 'but we can't be sure,' which sparked an outburst of laughter.

Cornish asked:

'As I'm now not driving back, thanks to Melanie's kind offer to take the wheel, I'd like to buy a round of drinks before we take our leave of you. Will you join us, gentlemen?'

'Alan, you're in Wales now,' Martin replied with a wry smile.

Cornish nodded. 'Yeah—that was a stupid question, wasn't it?'

Chapter 13

The pleasure was all mine

Probe's Offices, Cambridge Science Park, Milton Road, Cambridge

'Okay, let's take a step back for a moment and consider what we know so far.' Cornish leaned back in his chair and regarded Melanie and Zeezee with a smile as he tapped his fingertips together. A moment later he said:

'Firstly, we have a sixty-something-year-old murder and nobody has ever been charged. The main suspect was Vera Parsons because she was found in Weldon's office slumped over his dead body. And, being assessed as *unfit* to plead after his murder, she was never tried and never convicted. But, *finally,* after fifty-odd years, she has broken her silence—and even though she was sectioned for more than ten years, she has *denied* killing Weldon.'

'Do you agree, Melanie?'

'Yes—I do.'

Cornish continued. 'Secondly, after your further investigations interviewing Doris Harris, we've taken *her* off the suspect list?'

'That's correct. Doris had no motive and her means and opportunity were at best, *tenuous.*'

Cornish got to his feet and pointed to the prompt board behind him. 'And finally, the other suspects, Phillip Manson and nurse Sally Griffith are both dead, so we won't be interviewing them, will we? … So, unless you guys have some really good ideas about how to progress this case, I think it's time to drop it and get on with something that we have a *chance* of solving and, more importantly, getting paid for.'

Melanie looked concerned. 'But let's not forget something,' she said, 'we also have *another* unsolved and possibly *connected* murder.'

'Phillip Manson?' Cornish asked.

'Exactly!'

Silence filled the room.

'Zeezee, what's the chances of finding out who Phillip Manson really was?'

'I should have the full police file within the hour.'

'Good… Because until we know who he was there's not a lot we can do. Keep us informed Zeezee. We'll reconvene when you have something.'

Melanie and Zeezee got up and walked out the office. Zeezee headed off towards his desk.

'Melanie!' Cornish called out.

Melanie stopped and turned back.

'I forgot to thank you for driving back the other day.'

'And I forgot to thank you for the lovely evening meal and the lunch at the clubhouse. What was it called?'

'Rafters—and the pleasure was *all* mine.'

Sorry Alan, but you're wrong there—for a change, Melanie thought, as she headed back to her desk.

Cornish walked pensively back to his chair. *Sex at Six—it would have to be good to beat that steak,* he thought.

Chapter 14

And what about my milk and biscuits?

(Putney, London,1948)

'Don't be sad Porky, I promise I'll cum and visit yer.'

'But yer my only *real* friend, Jess!'

'You'll find someone else after I've gone.'

'Yeah, but what 'bout my milk and biscuits, Jess?'

'Ah, well, that might be a bit of a problem, I must admit.'

'Why do you 'ave to go anyway... I fort you was happy 'ere?'

Jess gazed at Porky's pleading expression and she knew she was going to miss him. But she couldn't tell him about what she'd done to Father Thomas and why she had to leave—not yet anyway. The police were questioning everyone about the incident but so far she'd managed to avoid them. She knew it was time to move on.

'I don't want to be doing this for the rest of my life, do I, Porky?—And all for a bloody *pittance!*' Jess placed the iron back on the coal-fired stove to heat it up again.

'So what yer gonna do then?' Porky asked, before downing the last of his glass of milk.

'I'm gonna be a nurse.'

'A nurse?—Get lost!'

'I am Porky, I'm gonna be a nurse in this new NHS fing; everyone's talking 'bout it and they need lots of nurses… Wipe yer north-un-south, will yer?'

Porky wiped his mouth with the sleeve of his shirt. 'What about yer family then?'

Jessica sighed. 'I 'en't got a family 'ave I.'

Porky frowned. 'You must've, Jess?'

'I 'en't got any; they was killed in the war they was.'

'That's sad Jess…But what 'bout yer bruvvers and sisters then?

'I don't 'ave any, do I.'

'We all got bruvvers and sisters.'

'I don't, Porky! *Okay*?' Jessica said, forcefully, but in her mind's eye she could see her half-brother, and the smirking face of the man who had the bloody nerve to call himself *Daddy*. Suddenly she could smell his smoky breath and feel his grubby hands probing her privates. She realised then how similar her half-brother and *Daddy* looked. Jessica's whole body stiffened. She closed her eyes and shook her head to clear her mind of the haunting images that refused to go away; unwelcome images that all-too-frequently clawed their way into her mind's eye during the cold, dark nights in her tiny attic room.

I should care 'bout my muvver, but I don't—and I don't feel guilty either, she mused.

Jessica's Irish mother, Mary, was a dark-haired, thin-framed woman with hard features, who looked much older than her thirty-five-years, thanks, in part, to her incessant pipe smoking and heavy drinking. She was well-known around the docklands area for her fiery Irish temper. Jessica, who looked like her father, had never felt any affection towards her mother and indeed had never received any affection from her; the only emotion Jessica felt for her mother was a festering *resentment*. Her mother had always been too-busy-to-do-this or too-busy-to-do-that and spent more time cleaning well-to-do people's houses rather than her own.

But what really sparked Jessica's resentment was not their loveless relationship but the fact that her mother *always* sided with *Daddy*. There was no point in telling Mother what *He'd* done to her; how he regularly defiled her, robbing her of her innocence. Her mother simply wouldn't have believed her *lies!*

'Sorry, Jess… Its none of my business anyways… So—can I cum with yer then? I'll be yer bruvver—as yer 'en't got one. You be the nurse and I'll be the doctor.'

Jess smiled at the pathetic creature *desperate* not to lose his best friend.

'…I don't fink yer family would be too happy 'bout that Porky…But don't worry, I'll cum back and see yer…I promise…*Porky*! Stop picking yer nose!

'Can I 'ave a nuvver biscuit then?'

'I dunno 'bout that…Yeah…go on, help yerself—and use the fingers what 'en't bin up yer nose.'

'Fanks Jess!' Porky pulled out the cork and shoved his hand in the glass jar knowing *exactly* where the biggest biscuit was.

'They've been up yer nose!'

'Shut up, they 'ent!'

Jess checked that the iron was hot enough again by raising it close to her cheek and then continued to press the bed sheets. She watched Porky as he devoured his second ginger biscuit and then she asked him:

'You still singing in the choir?'

'Yeah!—Miss Morgan's still in charge,' he said, and then he fell unusually silent.

'You okay, Porky?' Jessica asked after a few moments.

'Yeah...the new priest seems a lot nicer...I don't miss that *dirty* Father Thomas though! I'm *glad* he's dead. One of the boys in the choir told me that all that was left of 'im was his legs! How good is *that* Jess*?* But the coppers don't know who dunnit. If I knew who'd dunnit I'd fank 'im I would.'

Jess smiled contentedly. 'But you wouldn't share your biscuits with 'im, would yer?'

Porky shook his head. 'Nah!'

Jess laughed and continued with the ironing.

I am going to be a nurse. This East-End girl is going to make something of her life. The NHS is calling me. It's my destiny. I'm not stupid I can do it, I know I can.

'Porky, will yer promise me something?'

'What is it, Jess?'

'If yer gets asked about Father Thomas will yer be honest and tell them what he did to yer?'

Porky fell silent and pouted his bottom lip.

'It's 'portant, Porky. They need to know what he was like or there'll be more of 'em in the future. More perverts, hiding behind the banner of religion to practice their disgusting habits on young vulnerable children. Promise me Porky, or you'll never have another biscuit out of that jar.'

Porky forced a smile. 'I promise yer Jess—I'll tell 'em—if they asks me, okay?'

'Okay.'

'I won't get into trouble though will I?' Porky asked, frowning.

'Don't yer worry yer little brain 'bout that Porky, you haven't dun nuffink wrong, 'ave yer? You was an innocent victim, you was.'

Porky nodded, 'I was, yeah.'

Jessica vividly remembered the blade sinking into the priest's neck and the incredulous look on his moist face and the metallic smelling blood that spurted from his mouth, covering his face like a mask—a death mask.

Adrenalin began to surge through her veins again.

Chapter 15

He was his father's son

(East London, 1950)

'That's a lotta feckin ackers!'

'Roger my boy, if you want a *real* Sexton Blake qualification you've got to pay top-notch bangers-un-mash for it these days. This stuff comes with feckin *references* an all, my son. It's feckin good quality; look at it—check the details. A degree from a London university is worth a lot yer know.'

Roger Boardman unfolded the inscribed qualification bearing the name:

Phillip Henry Manson,

Inside the scroll was a folded birth certificate bearing the same name. The date of birth, written in black ink, was: 9, *June 1928*; Roger Boardman's actual birth date.

'So for a *nifty* my friend you have a *very* bright future ahead of yer, even if I say so myself.' The man opposite Boardman downed the dregs of his pint and placed his empty glass on the table. Smirking at his potential customer he said:

'Your round, I do believe?'

Boardman gazed nervously across the table at the smiling spiv with the greased-back hair and pencil-thin moustache. Boardman drained his pint and walked over to the bar.

The landlady asked:

'What can I get yer, luv?'

'Same again,' Boardman replied, looking straight through her.

'Same glasses, luv?'

'Yeah,' he said, clearly deep in thought. He tapped the end a *Senior Service* on its pack, lit it and inhaled deeply as he watched the landlady pulling the pints.

'That's one and sixpence, please, she said, placing the fresh pints on the polished-brass drip tray.'

Boardman's hands were noticeably shaking when he paid for the beer.

'You all right, luv?' the woman enquired.

'Yeah—gotta lot on my mind—okay!'

The landlady raised her hands. 'Okay! just asking.'

Boardman walked back to the table with the two beers.

'So, do we have a deal then, Roger?' the man asked before taking a long slurp of his fresh pint.

'... A nifty's a lot of feckin money for a degree certificate—is that yer best offer?'

'You're forgetting something mate, that price *includes* the birth certificate. Cum on, I'm already doing yer a feckin favour my son; have a strawberry tart. I've got a very demanding trouble and strife and six dustbin lids to keep yer know, and they ain't feckin cheap, I can tell yer.'

Boardman nodded thoughtfully, 'Tomorrow, in 'ere, seven o'clock; I'll 'ave the nifty with me.'

'That's the ammer my son! I look forward to seeing yer tomorrow then—*Phillip Manson,'* the spiv chuckled, gathered up the certificates and dropped them into his briefcase, then he picked up his drink and walked off with a contented swagger.

Roger Boardman sipped his pint and took a deep drag on his cigarette as he thought about how he was going to find the fifty pounds. He would need to choose his victims very carefully. They would have to be well-to-do people. No point in robbing a waif when you need cash. It was time to go up town, where the rich cunts lived. Soho was twenty minutes away by bus. He would start there. Lots of men with money looking for whores.

When Boardman arrived in Soho the sun had set some thirty minutes earlier and the women-of-the-night were beginning to appear on the streets. Dirty feckin trollops they were, rotting from the inside with gonorrhoea and syphilis, and far too old for Boardman. He wouldn't put his prick into a rotting whore.

She would have to be innocent, pure and *unadulterated*. That's what excited him, that's what made his prick rock hard.

Aylesbury Street was where he found his first victim. A man about forty, clearly intoxicated. Boardman chose his moment well just as the man reached Jerusalem Passage. He quickly looked around him; it was all clear. From under his coat he pulled out a black ebony truncheon, as hard as steel, and pushed the man into the lane, smashing the cosh down on his head with a sickening thud. The man fell to his knees as blood squirted from a deep gash on his head. The man moaned and flailed in agony but the second and third vicious blows from behind split his head wide open and knocked his false teeth out. Boardman's first victim was dead before his torso had slumped to the ground.

Boardman quickly emptied his victim's pockets and wiped the blood off the truncheon in the man's coat. He then casually walked away from the recumbent corpse, heading towards Compton Street; needing only another twenty-six pounds to reach his target.

Soon he would be able to leave the smog-bound city behind and start a new life far away from London as Phillip Henry Manson. He would become a respected psychologist with money to spend on clothes and a flashy car, but more importantly, on the things that raised him to another level of excitement; things that elevated him to the *upper* echelons of sexual arousal. The *forbidden* things he *craved* for and had to be so careful to keep *secret.*

He was his father's son.

It would be another thirty minutes before the sound of a woman's scream, followed by the piercing shrill of a policeman's whistle, announced the discovery of the mutilated body in Jerusalem Passage.

Unfortunately—by then—Roger Boardman's *next* victim had already been carefully selected. The well-to-do father of four who strode purposefully out of the gentleman's club smelling of perfume and expensive cigars was blissfully unaware that he had less than twenty minutes to live. In his wallet he had one hundred and thirty pounds.

Chapter 16

Death was obvious though

Zeezee walked back to Cornish's office twenty minutes later with further news. He knocked on the door and waited for the usual '*Come in,*' from Cornish.

'Come in… What have you got for us, Zeezee?'

'The news on Manson isn't good, I'm afraid. The original autopsy failed to produce anything that would reveal his real identity.'

Cornish picked up his phone. 'Melanie, pop in the office will you.'

A moment later Melanie walked in.

Cornish gestured to the seats. 'Sit down guys… It's not good news I'm afraid, Melanie.'

Zeezee repeated his words. 'The original autopsy failed to identify who he really was. No fingerprints or dental records to go on. Death was obvious though.'

Zeezee held up a photo of the corpse showing a long knife that had entered under his chin and protruded out of the top of his head by about twenty centimetres. 'No prints on the knife, obviously.'

Melanie cringed when she saw the black and white image. 'Oh my God!'

'One thing though, his fake qualifications were identified as coming from London. There were a lot of them produced after the war in the East End.'

'So that might be where he's from?' Melanie added. 'Do you know who produced them?'

'Too long ago now,' Zeezee said, shaking his head. 'Probably produced in some long-gone bombed out ruin somewhere.'

Cornish glanced at Melanie and she glanced back with a clearly despondent expression.

'What about his belongings, his home, wasn't there something there to give them a clue?' Cornish asked.

'His flat was searched but they didn't find anything out of the norm.'

'Any photo's of his family?' Melanie asked.

'None at all, just his fake certificate hanging on the wall of the living room. The strange thing is, within three week's of Weldon's death, Manson had departed Llanarth for good, and there's no record of him ever practicing psychology again—but that doesn't mean to say he didn't practice somewhere else in the world under a different name.'

Cornish tapped his fingertips together again; something he always did when an idea was materialising in his mind. '…Melanie, do you think it's worth a visit to see Vera again?'

'To talk about Manson?'

'Yeah, to ask her if there's *anything* she can remember that might help us identify him.'

Melanie smiled. 'It's worth a try, Alan, but I don't hold much hope.'

'I wasn't expecting to see you again, my dear,' Vera said settling down on the familiar bench in the garden.

Melanie sat down next to her. 'I hope you don't mind me intruding on your privacy again, Vera.'

'Not at all, it's nice to see a different face now and again. I'd rather look at you than that old cow in there. She's still wearing that bloody death mask. It'll be worn out before she snuffs it,' Vera giggled. 'So what exactly do you want to know this time, *Melanie*? That's right isn't it?'

'Yes, that's right, Vera… Melanie Underwood. Well, we're still investigating the murder of Doctor Anthony Weldon.'

'Really! Have you made any progress?'

'Some, but not enough if I'm honest, Vera.'

'Well, it was a long time ago now, wasn't it?'

'Yes, it was. I actually went to visit Doris Harris the other day.'

'Doris Harris! I thought she was dead.'

'No, she's *very* much alive. What made you think she was dead?'

Vera looked puzzled. 'I was convinced she'd died of an overdose, but obviously I was wrong.'

'We've ruled her out of our investigation. Nurse Sally Griffith is dead though. She died of cancer some years ago.'

'So none of the suspects are alive?' Vera asked.

'That's right, but we are interested to know more about Phillip Manson.'

'He was murdered wasn't he?'

'Yes, he was, Vera.'

'And you're going to ask me if I know anyone who had a reason to kill him.'

'I am. We're also interested to find out his *real* identity; Phillip Manson wasn't his real name.'

'People at Llanarth didn't like him. He was arrogant and very often rude to the patients—but that wasn't justification to kill him of course. I can't imaging anyone at Llanarth doing such a thing. Anyway he was killed somewhere else wasn't he, not at Llanarth?'

Melanie nodded. 'He was killed in York…Vera, can you think of *anything* he might of done or said to suggest where he might have come from?'

Vera was quiet for some time, deep in thought. 'No, not really. He had a posh accent so I think he must have come from a monied family.'

'And yet he had a false identity.'

'Yes, that's true. Maybe he was a clever con-man then, cos he certainly fooled me.'

'Not just you Vera… So you can't remember him saying *anything* about where he came from?'

'I'm sorry my dear, my memory's not what it used to be.'

'Don't worry, Vera. It was a long shot anyway.'

'The one thing I really remember about him is that he took my lover *away* from me and I hated him for it.'

'What do you mean, took him away, Vera?'

'…You know…down the pub all the *fucking* time.'

'Ah! I see,' said Melanie.

Chapter 17

Why would she stay silent?

'I wasn't expecting to get any answers, if I'm honest, Alan,' Melanie said, putting her glass of wine down on the table.

'That's the name of the game we're in, I'm afraid,' Cornish sighed, despondently, 'I needed a beer tonight. Thanks for joining me, Melanie. I hope you didn't mind me asking you?'

'*Why* should I mind?'

Cornish smiled and sipped his drink as he gazed into Melanie's sparkling eyes. 'It's beautiful isn't it?' he said.

'What is?'

'I could sit here next to the river for hours watching the world go by. It's so bloody peaceful.'

Melanie sat quietly listening to Alan; content to be in his company again.

'You know, Melanie, something that Vera said is *really* bugging me.'

'Tell me more,' she prompted, 'I'm intrigued.'

'Well,… Vera's world imploded when she found Weldon's body—Correct?'

'That's right—she said her brain switched off like a computer.'

'So how come Vera knew that Doris's door had been left open the night of the murder? She said to you, and I quote: "*The morning after Tony had been murdered it was reported that Doris's door had been unlocked all night.*" Now, if Vera had *switched off,* like she so vividly described to you, then she wouldn't have had a *clue* about the door being left open, would she? According to her she'd already turned into a silent zombie by then!'

Melanie sipped her wine as she gazed back into Cornish's eyes.

'A silent zombie,' she repeated. 'So you think she's lying about why she fell silent for all those years? Now you mention it she did make a comparison between her and Weldon and Antony and Cleopatra and when I looked surprised she said: "Not much else to do with my time, I'm afraid,"'

'I believe she's playing a game with us.'

Melanie asked: 'But why would she stop talking?'

'Obviously to protect someone,' interjected Cornish, confidently. 'And another thing, how did she know that Manson had been killed. It wasn't exactly common knowledge down south, was it?'

'Okay,' Melanie continued, 'let's *assume* Manson killed Weldon and Vera knew he was the murderer. Weldon was her *lover* and therefore the only reason she would stay silent *and* take the *rap* for it was… because…?'

Cornish answered: 'Because, for some reason, she was *protecting* Manson.'

'…But why?'

'That, Melanie, is a very good question…a question I need to sleep on… Shall we eat out here, it's so nice tonight?'

'Yeah why not, but it's *my* shout this evening.'

Cornish leaned over the bench and took Melanie's hand. 'I asked you out and you were kind enough to say yes… I'm paying—okay?'

'Okay, Melanie conceded.'

'Sitting here with you by the river, on such a *beautiful* evening as this, makes all the long hours and frustrating setbacks just that little bit more bearable.'

Oh God, that was a compliment! 'Thank you.'

'You're welcome.'

'So what do you fancy to eat, Alan?'

'I'm going for the oysters. You know what they say.'

'Alan!'

Cornish laughed and finished off his pint. Come on, drink up. Melanie finished her wine and handed him her glass.

'Same again?'

Melanie smiled. 'Why not?—I'm not driving tonight.'

'So obviously you live not far from here?'

'A ten minute walk down the river, at Riverside Place. But don't forget *you* are driving, Alan.'

'…I can always get a taxi to Trumpington if need be. Let's just enjoy it while we can.'

Melanie smiled. *That won't be difficult.*

Two hours passed in an instant. Melanie and Cornish stopped talking shop and began to get to know each other on a personal level.

Cornish, after a few beers opened up about his past relationship with a woman who had been killed on the M6 in a multiple-pile-up some ten-years-ago. Since that time, he admitted to Melanie, work had become his first priority. He had not allowed a new relationship to get in the way of his *dream*.

Melanie, with the courage gained from a few glasses of wine, admitted that her parents were extremely rich.

Her father was a self-taught investment entrepreneur and had made his fortune on the stock market. Some of his high-risk ventures in Asia and China had paid out handsomely. Much of his wealth now resided in the hands of reputable fund managers, allowing him to enjoy a less stressful life struggling to play to his single-figure golf handicap. Melanie's mother always insisted that he just got lucky, but Melanie knew her father was much more than just 'lucky.' She reminded Cornish that he'd seen her mother and father at the charity event three year's earlier when Cornish offered her the job there and then.

Cornish raised a finger 'I remember them. The best decision I've everrrr made,' he added.

'Alan, you're beginning to slur your words.'

'Am I? Oh God!—I'm sorry, Melanie.'

Melanie reached over and held his hand. 'It's okay, there's no need to apologise. But I think it's time to go, don't you?'

'Yeah, you're right. I'll pay the bill and call for a taxi.'

Melanie smiled. 'Alan, please don't take this the wrong way but you're welcome to stay at my place tonight—in the *guest* room. We can walk there in ten minutes and you can pick your car up in the morning.'

Cornish returned the smile. 'A walk beside the river with you sounds rather appealing. Thank you—I accept your kind offer, young lady,' he said, and saluted.

Oh Alan, you are so sweet.

Cornish paid the bill and they walked out onto the tree-lined Riverside. He offered his arm and Melanie cheerfully wrapped hers around it. The evening was still and peaceful, apart from the occasional cyclist and late-evening jogger.

For a while they walked together in silence, arm-in-arm, looking at the colourful narrowboats moored up along the riverbank with their pretty pots of flowers and herbs adorning their cabin roofs. Some even had smoke rising from their chimneys, which hung like a magic carpet in the still night air above them. The sweet smell reminded Melanie of her childhood and the log fires at Christmas time.

The sumptuousness of Melanie's penthouse apartment, overlooking the River Cam, took Cornish by surprise. The furnishings were clearly expensive, and tasteful, creating a relaxed welcoming feel to the place. In the far corner of the lounge stood a magnificent black grand piano. Cream leather sofas surrounded a central wood-burner and an open-tread stairs led up to the three, second-floor bedrooms, main bathroom and mini gym. Up another level there was a large roof-top garden filled with lush bamboo, leafy banana plants and colourful well-stocked raised flower beds. A large table and chairs nestled under a huge, rectangular Veuve Clicquot parasol and of course there was the inevitable gas barbecue. The *only* thing Melanie's place had in common with Cornish's little terraced house, across town in Trumpington, was the barbecue.

Cornish looked down over the rooftop balcony at the shimmering river below—he was still in awe of the place.

Melanie arrived carrying two glasses of bubbly and handed him one. 'It's only rented, it's not mine.'

'It's still fantastic…This stuff makes my legs very wobbly,' he slurred, and Melanie giggled.

'They're already very wobbly, Alan,' Melanie pointed out and they both laughed. 'Cheers,' she said, chinking their glasses.

'Cheers…and thank you so much Melanie,' he managed; intoxicated with drink and the sheer beauty of the woman standing next to him. 'I've had…(hick) I've had a *wonderful* time… tonight.'

You're such a lovely, man…I really want you to kiss me… but you won't will you, you stubborn mule. Why not?I know you like me. Maybe I should kiss you?…

No,—that might not be a good idea—Not tonight, she thought.

Melanie was lying naked on the bed, aware that Alan was in the next bedroom and the thought was keeping her awake. On her bedside table her iPhone was playing a *Lady Antebellum* song and Melanie quietly joined in, singing:

I*t's a quarter after one*
I'm all alone and I need you now
And I said I wouldn't call
but I'm a little drunk and I need you now
And I don't know how I can do without
I just need you now

'I couldn't have said it better myself,' she whispered.

Alan was lying in bed in the guest room deep in thought, trying to work out why Vera Parsons would want to protect a piece of shit like the charlatan Phillip Manson. He mused about Vera and he realised he knew very little about Manson *or* her. It was clear to him that to understand the situation better they would have to know more about Manson and Vera. And then within a matter of minutes he'd drifted into a restless sleep.

Chapter 18

We need to find out more about Vera

'Tea or coffee?' Melanie called out from the kitchen.

'Tea please!' came the response from the guest room.

Melanie measured three scoops of loose-leaf tea into the teapot and poured in some boiling water. 'Bacon and eggs!?'she called out.

'Oh, yes please,' Cornish answered as he walked down the stairs.

'Sorry, I didn't mean to shout. I thought you were still in your room.'

Cornish walked into the kitchen and Melanie surprised him with a kiss on the cheek. 'Good morning, did you sleep well?'

Cornish nodded. '…Yeah, I did, thank you…I got a bit drunk last night didn't I? Please tell me I didn't embarrass myself?'

Melanie smiled and passed him a mug of steaming tea. 'You were fine,' she said, with an air of affection in her voice, 'Sugar and milk are on the table, help yourself… Fried or boiled?'

'Fried, please.'

'Two enough?'

'Plenty, thanks… Oh my God! …This tea is wonderful.'

'Loose-leaf English Breakfast tea, fresh water, warm pot, let it stand; what could be simpler?'

'This place is lush, Melanie.' Cornish walked over to the grand piano and stroked the polished lid, thinking about the kiss on his cheek. 'Do you play?'

'Yes, I do, but not enough any more I'm afraid; mostly classical stuff.'

'Nice—I'm more into rock, myself.' Cornish lifted the lid and pressed a white key. 'Lovely sound, but then it is a *Steinway*.'

'A gift from my parents for my twenty-first birthday.'

'Very nice.'

'Come and sit down, breakfast is ready.'

Cornish joined her at the table and eagerly tucked into his bacon and eggs while Melanie topped up his mug.

'My mind was working overtime last night,' he said.

I know the feeling, she thought.

'We need to know more about Vera.'

'Yes, I agree,' Melanie said. 'All we really know is she's the last surviving member of a large family from Canterbury. Her father died in the war and her mother struggled to bring them up.'

'Let's get Zeezee to check her story out. I'm not sure I trust her.'

'Why would she lie about her roots?'

'Because she's hiding something?' Cornish suggested.

'Possibly.'

'Melanie, we need to get all of our ducks in a row if we're going to solve this mystery... By the way—I love your slippers.'

Melanie looked down at her Minnie Mouse slippers. 'I only wear them on special occasions.'

Cornish laughed, then admitted: 'I really enjoyed last night... I have a vague recollection of drinking bubbly on the roof.'

'Yes, we did.'

'It's no wonder I was drunk.'

'And you *insisted* that we get *naked!*'

Cornish's mouth dropped open. *'What!'*

'Only joking!'

'Christ!' Cornish rubbed his temples. 'Don't do that to me!' he said, smirking. 'You really had me going there for a moment.'

Melanie grinned. 'You are funny.'

'I can't take too much of that bubbly, Melanie.'

'I think the damage was already done by then, Alan.'

Cornish giggled. 'Yeah, you're probably right.'

'Toast and marmalade?'

'You're spoiling me... and I love it,' he said, checking his watch. 'I'll walk back to get the car after breakfast. The fresh air will help clear my head. I'll see you later in the office and then I'll explain what I think we need to do to progress this—but one thing's for sure.'

'What's that?'

Cornish stopped buttering his toast for a moment and said: 'We'll need to get permission from the coroner to exhume Manson's body, and that Melanie, is not going to be easy. They'll want a very good reason for doing it. Did you get Vera's cigarette butt?'

'Yes, I did, on my last visit. I gave it to Forensics.'

'Good,' he said, and continued to butter his toast.

Melanie smiled and pondered. *Alan Cornish, what are you up to?*

Later at Probe's Offices, Cornish said;

'Zeezee, I want you to do some digging for me.' Cornish got up and walked around his desk to the middle of the office. He turned and looked at Melanie. 'I think our Vera is telling us a load of pork pies.'

Melanie considered his words. 'I think she has been honest about Weldon, because Doris confirmed it.'

'Okay then, let's assume she was his lover. I need to know who she *really* is... and who the hell Manson really was. Zeezee, check out her story about growing up in Canterbury: father dying in the war, large family brought up by the mother, blah blah blah. I have a theory, do you want to hear it, guys?'

Zeezee and Melanie nodded expectantly.

'I believe that they are related. Weldon found out about Manson's fake qualifications and confronted him, so Manson killed him to shut him up, and Vera took the rap for her *brother*. Buy the way Melanie, you'll be pleased to hear Forensics got a good DNA sample from Vera's cigarette.'

Melanie smiled. 'But no match?'

'Unfortunately not; Vera's not on the database.'

'What we need now is a DNA sample from Manson's remains; but that won't be a certainty after nearly half a century in the ground.'

'And where are his remains?' Melanie asked.

'In a churchyard ten miles outside of York,' Zeezee confirmed.

Cornish continued. The test would tell us if they are siblings or whether my theory is *completely* wrong and they're not related at all.

'And do you have a theory as to *who* killed Manson, Alan?' Melanie asked.

'Not at this moment in time, Melanie, but the *more* we know about these two the better. My brain works a bit like a jig-saw puzzle and at the moment there's too many pieces missing for me to even see what the picture's really about. Zeezee, give it your best shot.'

'I'm on the case, boss,' he said, and strode out of the office.

Cornish gazed at Melanie. 'That was some breakfast.'

'How's your head?'

'I'll survive.'

'That's good,' she said, and went to walk out.

'Melanie…Thanks for letting me stay.'

'My pleasure; I enjoyed your company.'

'And I enjoyed yours. It's been a long time, too long if I'm honest, since I felt so relaxed. It's been all work and no play and last night I was letting off some stream. I didn't mean to get that drunk.'

'There's no need to apologise Alan, you were fine.'

'You're very understanding. Can we… Is it…Can we do it again, sometime?'

'…Yes, I'd *really* like that,' she said, and headed back to her desk with a broad grin on her face. *It must have been the tea,* she thought in jest.

Cornish returned to his desk and eased into his chair. He was smiling too. 'Best cuppa tea I've ever tasted,' he said to himself.

One hour later Zeezee returned to Cornish's office.

'I've run all the checks, Alan. Vera Parsons is not from Canterbury.'

'I knew it!' Cornish said, emphatically.

'I can find no record of her being born there.'

'That's because she's *not* from Canterbury and she's *not* Vera Parsons.'

'So who is she?' Zeezee asked.

'Why don't we just go and ask her?'

Cornish picked up the phone and tapped a speed dial button… 'Melanie, can you join us in my office please?'

When Melanie walked in, Cornish said: 'Guess what?—Zeezee can't find any record of Vera Parsons being born in Canterbury.'

'So why is she lying to me about where she's from?'

'She's *hiding* something, Melanie.'…Cornish started tapping his fingers together.

Melanie frowned. 'Maybe she's hiding something from us and *herself*—something *traumatic* like physical abuse; that's always a strong contender.'

'…Will you take me to see her?' Cornish asked.

Melanie nodded. 'If you think it will do any good; and *if* she agrees to see you, then *yes*, of course.'

'Before we see Vera I'm going make a call to the Yorkshire Police's Murder Investigation Unit to see if they will release any possible materials that would allow us to do a DNA test on Manson; that way we won't need to dig him up. After all the case-file is still open. We'll have to foot the bill but we can use our forensic friends at Copeland and Associates to do the DNA tests for us. We can then prove one-way-or-another that they're *definitely* related or that I'm *totally* wrong on this one.'

Melanie nodded. 'How long will that take to get the results if we're lucky enough to get a suitable sample?'

'Normally it would take a good few weeks to get the results back but I might be able to pull a few strings with our friends at Copeland and Associates.' Cornish winked at Melanie and then picked up his desk phone and his first call was to the Homicide Division at Yorkshire Police's Headquarters to speak with the Senior Investigating Office.

Chapter 19

Lex talionis—The law of retaliation

(London Paddington, 1952)

Roger Boardman stepped up onto the train at Paddington Station wearing a trilby hat, grey suit and a white shirt and tie. He was carrying, in one hand, a black leather briefcase and in the other hand, a new suitcase containing his sole belongings.

Tomorrow morning he would be meeting a Dr. Weldon at Llanarth Court in South Wales for an interview as a junior clinical psychologist under his new guise as Phillip Manson.

Boardman's last two weeks had been spent in libraries near the Thames reading up on psychology; especially Sigmund Freud with his *new* method of psychoanalysis for treating psychopathology, through dialogue, between a patient and a psychoanalyst.

He was confident he could blag his way through the interview. He was intelligent and good at bullshitting, and with his natural air of confidence he was sure the job would be his. He was determined never to come back to this smog-bound shit-hole.

Weldon was a medical doctor, he wasn't a psychologist, and Freud's new technique was *revolutionary*. It was all about sitting down with a feckin *nutter* and talking to 'im. What a load of feckin bullshit! What could be *easier* than that?

Nice to meet you Phillip. Nice to meet you Doctor Weldon and thank you for offering me the position of junior psychologist. I'm sure you'll be delighted to know Doctor Weldon that I accept your kind offer. Boardman sniggered, enjoying his role-play scenario; pleased with his new accent. He lit a Capstan Full Strength and settled back into the seat, smiling broadly.

The guard's shrill whistle blew and the engine, shrouded in steam, hissed and belched dark smoke into the air as it slowly pulled its reluctant carriages away from the platform, heading west into the golden afternoon sun.

Boardman lifted his suitcase onto the rack above him and settled back into his second-class seat in the otherwise empty compartment. He opened his briefcase and took out his notebook and Weldon's letter inviting him to the interview and explaining a little of what would be expected of him if he was offered the position. Boardman re-read the letter for the seventh time.

It was time to revisit his copious hand-written notes and the case studies he would *briefly* mention in the interview, hoping-beyond-hope that Weldon would not want to go into too much detail. As he read he enunciated slowly and clearly.

In his briefcase was the fake qualification and birth certificate he'd bought at a cost of fifty pounds—plus the lives of two middle-aged men and one nineteen-year-old prostitute. Boardman had already heard the rumour on the street that the young prostitute's notorious gangland pimp was intent on seeking revenge for his loss of earnings.

'Of all the feckin whores in London I had to choose Ronnie's whore,' he said to himself. He knew Ronnie of old and remembered him standing at the bar in the pub laughing and joking one day, less than an hour after he'd shot a bloke in the head, and preaching to his faithful gang of followers, saying: 'Lex talionis my boys—lex talionis.'

Ronnie Molinari was not a man to mess with.

There was no way back for Roger Boardman—and he knew it.

Chapter 20

My name is Vera Parsons

(Abergavenny, South Wales, 1952)

The following morning the sun was shining

when Boardman walked out of the Angel Hotel on Cross Street to meet the taxi driver waiting for him at the entrance.

'Are you Mister Mansel, sir?'

'The name is *Manson.*'

'Sorry sir, I believe you want's to go to Llanarth Court is that right, Mister *Manson*?'

'Yes, that's right, I have a *very* important meeting there at ten o'clock.'

The taxi driver placed Manson's suitcase in the boot of the black cab and slammed it shut, he then opened the rear door of the cab and said:

'Hop in then, sir, I'll have you there with time to spare.'

'Good,' replied Boardman, tersely.

The taxi moved off and Boardman settled into the back seat talking quietly to himself.

'You a doctor then sir?' the driver asked.

'Psychologist, actually,' Boardman replied.

'What's that all about then, sir?'

'I study the human mind, and try to understand the reasons for certain kinds of behaviour. I am a strong advocate of the pioneering works of Sigmund Freud.'

'Oh… I see… You've gone and lost me there I'm afraid, sir, cy— cy—'

'Psychologist… Please, just drive, I have work to do before I get there, Boardman said, impatiently.'

'Right oh, sir, sorry sir.'

Twenty minutes later the taxi drove through the arched-stone gatehouse of Llanarth Court and continued along the long, meandering drive towards the manor house.

'There it is, sir,' the driver said, as the house came into view. Boardman peered out through the windscreen, shocked at the size of the place. 'Christ! It's a country house. Are you sure you've got the right address?'

The driver chuckled. 'Quite sure! It was a *gift* to the Roman Catholic Church would you believe, sir; four years-ago now. As if *they* needed it with *all* their bloody wealth, I ask you? God knows why they didn't give it to me,' the cabby said, laughing, 'it's just the right size for me and the missus.'

But the taxi driver's humour was waisted on Boardman who was staring straight ahead, deep in thought, wiping his clammy palms on his suit trousers.

What have I gone and done?

'This place has a lovely lake, too,' the driver said, pointing to his right, 'but my mate, who's a really keen fisherman, tells me that it's silting up badly now, sir. Bit of a shame really, I s'pose. Still, he won't be fishing here anymore, now that it's a nut house, will he, sir?'

Roger Boardman didn't hear a single word of the driver's conversation.

'Here we are sir,' said the driver stopping outside the main entrance. 'Will you be requiring my services later on in the day?'

'No,' Boardman replied, 'I won't—I'm going to be working here.'

When Boardman stepped out of the taxi he noticed a tall, dark-haired man standing at the entrance to the building. *That must be Weldon,* he thought.

'That's three shillings then please, sir,' said the taxi driver as he lifted Boardman's suitcase out of the boot.

Boardman handed the driver four shilling coins and walked off towards the main entrance.

The taxi driver touched his cap and said:

'Much obliged to you Mister Mansel.'

'Phillip Manson I presume?' Doctor Weldon said, holding out his hand and smiling as Boardman approached.

'And you must be Doctor Weldon?' Boardman responded, shaking hands confidently with the doctor.

'That's me, but call me Tony, please. *Welcome* to Llanarth Court, Phillip.'

Boardman looked relaxed as he gazed up at the house's elegant three layered facade but inside him, his heart was pounding. 'What a magnificent place this is,' he said, quietly pleased with his new persona.

'Yes, not a bad place to work, is it?'

'The air is so fresh.'

'Yes— and somewhat of a *contrast* to the London smog I would suggest, Phillip.'

'And such a *pleasant* contrast too, Doctor,' Boardman confirmed, nodding.

'How was your journey?' Weldon asked gesturing to the main entrance.

'Quite relaxing really; I travelled up yesterday by train and stayed at the Angel Hotel in Abergavenny last night.'

'And how did they treat you?'

'No complaints at all; I slept well and breakfast was excellent.'

In reality Boardman was so nervous he hardly slept at all and only managed one piece of buttered toast and a cup of tea before he left the hotel.

Weldon smiled. 'That's good; I've stayed there myself on a number of occasions but since last year I now live in. This post also includes accommodation here of course.'

'Yes, that is very appealing I must say.'

'Don't get too excited, the accommodation is *pretty* basic I'm afraid. Just a single room on the top floor in fact, but it's clean and tidy and all your meals are provided seven day's a week in the canteen; all of which is reflected in the renumeration package. As you may have gathered by now we are a bit isolated here; it's not like London.'

That's what I wanted to hear, thought Boardman as they walked.

'I'll be very honest with you Phillip, you are the only one to have applied for the post so far. I guess we have the war to thank for that.'

Boardman felt a tingle of excitement as they entered the building and ascended a magnificent sweeping staircase to the second floor.

Weldon pointed up and said:

'The stairs continue up to the staff bedrooms but this is my office on the left.' Weldon opened the door that carried the name *Dr. Anthony Weldon* in gold lettering and gestured to Manson to enter. 'Hang your hat and coat on the stand, take a seat and make yourself comfortable whilst I'll go and get some tea and biscuits organised.'

Boardman hung his hat and coat on the stand behind the door and settled on a chair in front of Weldon's desk. He glanced nervously around the room at the numerous medical books on the shelves and fidgeted with his uncomfortably stiff collar.

A moment later there was a knock on the office door and a pretty young nurse walked in smiling. But her smile soon vanished and the blood drained from her face when she looked at Boardman.

'Well, well! If it isn't my *murderous* little sister, Jessica!'

'…I'm afraid you're very *mistaken*, sir, my name is Vera Parsons,' she stressed, anxiously. 'I'm a nurse here.'

'And your loving brother's name is now Philip Manson. Pleased to meet you, Vera.' His insipid grin, so reminiscent of his father's, chilled her blood.

A moment later Weldon returned carrying a tray of tea and biscuits. 'Ah! Nurse Parsons I see you've met Phillip Manson. Phillip has applied to work here as a junior clinical psychologist.'

'How do you do, sir?' Vera said, weakly.

Boardman stood up, bowed his head and said: 'Very pleased to meet you, Nurse Parsons,'

'Are you okay, nurse?' Weldon asked. 'You look very pale.'

'I suddenly feel somewhat faint to be honest. I think I'll go and lie down for a while…Please excuse me.'

'Yes, of course, nurse. I'll call by your room a little later to see how you are, if that's all right with you?'

Vera didn't answer.

'Lovely to meet you Nurse Parsons,' Boardman called out as she walked a little unsteadily out of the room, forcefully closing the door behind her.

Weldon tutted and sighed. 'I don't know—women —there's always *something* wrong with them, isn't there? I'm just glad I'm a man.'

Manson nodded… 'Yes, I agree with you whole-heartedly, Doctor; they are most definitely the *weaker* sex.'

Vera staggered down the corridor clasping her heaving chest.

'No, no, no!—Please *God,* don't let this happen to me! Haven't I *suffered* enough?' she wailed in utter despair as the strength drained from her legs.

Chapter 21

I'm sure you'll work it out in time

Alan Cornish parked his car in one of the visitor's slots and looked across at Melanie. 'At least she's agreed to see me; that's a start.'

'So what exactly do you want to achieve today, Alan?'

Cornish took a deep breath. 'I want to find out who she really is and if she admits to Manson being her brother.'

'And just how do you intend to do that?'

'I don't know yet,' he said, 'it really depends on how she reacts to me. But don't worry Melanie, I'm not going in feet first. I want you to take control of the meeting because she trusts you and the last thing I want to do is spoil the relationship you've developed with her.'

'Okay,' Melanie said.

'Come on! Let's go and meet Vera.'

Cornish and Melanie exited the car and walked the short distance to the nursing home's main entrance. As they arrived the main door opened and the familiar overweight carer greeted them with a smile.

'Hello again Miss Underwood,' she said.

'Hello Carol. This is my colleague, Alan Cornish.'

Cornish stepped forward and shook the carer's hand.

'Pleased to meet you,' he said, and watched the carer's complexion turn a bright pink.

'Pleased to meet you, I'm sure.'

Melanie glanced at Cornish and raised her eyes.

'As it looks like rain today I think it might be better to see Vera in the visitor's room. It's quiet in there and I'll make sure you're not disturbed.'

'That's very kind of you.'

'It's no problem Miss Underwood. Can I get you a pot of tea?'

'That would be lovely, thank you.'

The carer showed them into a room that had plain magnolia coloured walls. A mix of conference chairs and armchairs were placed around the perimeter and an oversized glass-topped coffee table dominated a central position.

Once the carer had left them alone Cornish said: 'Christ! How depressing is this? The place smells of urine and boiled cabbage.'

Melanie nodded knowingly. 'That's why Vera and I talk in the garden; it's lovely out there. It's just a shame the weather's not so good today.'

After a few minutes the carer arrived arm-in-arm with Vera Parsons. Melanie walked towards her and took her hand. 'Hello Vera.'

'Hello my dear, how are you?'

'I'm very well, thank you. Vera I'd like to introduce you to my colleague, Alan Cornish.'

Cornish walked forward and offered his hand to Vera. 'Nice to meet you Miss Parsons.'

'Colleague *and* lover?' Vera asked, winking at Melanie.

This time it was Melanie's turn to blush.

'You're a good looker aren't you,' Vera said, shaking Cornish's hand.

Cornish was clearly taken aback by Vera's forthright manner. '…It's very kind of you to say so, Miss Parsons.'

'Tell him Melanie.'

Melanie looked at Cornish. 'You need to drop the *Miss Parsons* bit…Go with Vera.'

'My apologies, *Vera.*' Cornish added.

'You're forgiven, handsome.'

The carer raised her eyes and tutted. 'I'll go and get the tea then,' she said, 'and please behave yourself in front of your guests, Vera.'

'And leave some of the biscuits for us—you're fat enough as it is,' Vera responded; pointing a finger at the carer's extremely rotund belly.

Cornish glanced at Melanie who responded with an embarrassed tight-lipped smile and raised eyebrows.

'Help me into the seat, my dear.'

Melanie grasped Vera's arm and lowered her into an armchair. The old lady adjusted her skirt and made herself comfortable. Finally she said: 'I was right about her death mask, young lady. She snuffed it two day's ago.'

Melanie responded: 'Oh!—How sad!'

'Nonsense! We won't *miss* her at all; she was brain-dead anyway. Her only contribution to any conversation was cabbage smelling flatulence!'

Cornish smiled wondering how to approach this fiery old lady who clearly had her very own force-field in place. Getting through it was not going to be easy.

Cornish looked at Melanie and prompted her with a nod.

Melanie said:

'Vera, some-time-ago you told me that you were brought up in a big family by your mother, in Canterbury.'

'Did I?' The old lady replied, 'well, it must be true then.'

'But it's not true is it Vera?' Melanie added, sympathetically.

Vera smiled. 'I told you I didn't kill him and that was true.'

'We believe that you didn't kill Doctor Weldon,' Melanie added.

'Your *brother* killed Doctor Weldon, didn't he?' Cornish suggested.

Vera raised her hands to her mouth. '…What does it matter? They're both dead anyway,' she said, with an air of despondency.

'Phillip Manson was your brother, wasn't he, Vera?'

Vera's eyes filled with tears.

'And you took the blame for him. To protect him from the hangman.'

Vera nodded. 'How do you know all this?' she asked.

Cornish continued: 'Doctor Weldon found out about your brother's fake qualifications and your brother killed him to silence him, didn't he?'

Vera nodded. Tears trickled down her powder-puffed cheeks.

'So… if your brother wasn't really Phillip Manson, who was he? And more importantly, who are you, Vera? What's your real name?'

Suddenly the door swung open and the carer walked in carrying a tray.

Not again, thought Melanie.

'I've left you a couple of biscuits,' she said and placed the tray on the coffee table before striding out.

'Are you okay Vera?' Melanie asked, reaching for her hand.

The old lady nodded and dabbed under her eyes with a small lace handkerchief that smelled of cologne.

'…You're right, he was my brother,' she finally admitted, 'and I loved him with all my heart. I couldn't *bear* to see him hang for his crime; so I did what I had to do — for *him;* and I don't regret it, because he meant *the world* to me.'

Cornish smiled knowingly at Melanie and she smiled back.

'So what was your brother's real name, Vera?' Cornish asked.

'Oh, I'm sure you'll work it out in time, h*andsome,*' she said, confidently and proceeded to pour herself a cup of coffee.

Chapter 22

We know that failure of the psychosexual development can lead to neurosis, homosexuality and paedophilia.

(Llanarth Court, Monmouthshire, South Wales 1952)

Doctor Weldon reached over his desk and lit Phillip Manson's cigarette. 'Before we start, Phillip, let me explain what is going on here at Llanarth Court. This place was gifted to the Roman Catholic Church back in 1948 by the Honourable Fflorens Roch. I think Fflorens is Welsh for Florence, but don't quote me on that. She was from a well-to-do family in Monmouth I believe, not far from here. The Church decided to run it as a Benedictine School so you'll find a lot of monks dressed in black scurrying about the place but they're harmless enough and they keep themselves to themselves. Our government, however, has seconded the place for an *undermined* period of time, until proper hospital facilities become available. It's because of this new National Health Service thing that Aneurin Bevan announced in forty-eight. A wonderful idea but God knows how it's going to work. I have been given the job of setting up a team of medical staff capable of running both a secure and rehab unit. Luckily we've had our own canteen fitted because a life living on bread, porridge and prayers is not my idea of fun.'

'No, nor mine,' Manson agreed.

'So…We have a mix of mental and disabled patients, mostly ex-soldiers with a few women as well. Six males are in the new secure-unit and are considered highly dangerous, but don't worry we have strict rules in place for dealing with them. My superiors have promised me another trainee doctor, a psychiatrist, a psychologist and, the reason you're here today, a junior psychologist. The plan is to have everyone in place over the next few months but I'm not sure if that timescale will be achievable.'

Manson smiled politely, listening intently to Weldon.

'If you join us you'll be part of a start-up team and that can be great fun—if we get it right.'

'Sounds like an exciting challenge, Doctor.' Manson said, enthusiastically.

'I'd like to think so Phillip, but what I can't tell you is how long we'll actually be *here* at Llanarth Court for.'

Manson shrugged. 'I understand,' he said.

'So, that's enough about us for now, let's hear a bit about you and what you want to achieve.'

Manson leaned forward and pressed his cigarette into the ashtray on Weldon's desk. '…I want to be at the front lines, so to speak, gaining experience and learning from my superiors. Theory is all well and good but there is no substitute for hands-on experience.'

Weldon nodded in agreement.

'As you may have noticed I'm a keen follower of Sigmund Freud.'

'Yes, I gathered that,' Weldon said. 'Why is that, Phillip?'

Manson stroked his chin for effect. '…I strongly believe in the power of *communication* and Freud's approach to psychoanalysis is based on communication. I also believe his formulation of the Oedipus Complex in 1899 was *pivotal* to psychoanalytical theory and psychosexual development.'

Weldon nodded. 'Very interesting, and of course we know that *failure* of the psychosexual development can lead to neurosis, homosexuality and pedophilia.'

Manson smiled and nodded. 'Precisely, Doctor,' he said, confidently; but in truth he was completely unaware of the fact.

Chapter 23

Is this really happening to me?

(Llanarth Court 1952)

'How's the patient?' Weldon asked.

Vera managed a thin smile from her bed. 'I'm okay, Tony.'

'You looked like you'd seen a ghost, my love.'

Vera huffed and thought: *How ironic is that?*

Weldon placed his hand on her forehead. 'You don't seem to have a temperature.'

'I'll be okay... How did you get on with that Manson chap?'

'Oh, he's not ideal but he certainly has plenty of enthusiasm.'

'Surely you're not going to employ him, are you?'

'Why on Earth not?'

'I don't like the look of him?'

'He can't help the way he looks, Vera.'

'He looks dodgy. I wouldn't trust him, Tony.'

'I think you're over reacting, my love.'

'You're making a *big* mistake if you take him on, believe me.'

Weldon considered her words for a moment. 'I don't have any other options at the moment—he's the only one to apply for the job. I've told him I'll take him on for six weeks and then review the situation after that. If he's no good and proves to be *dodgy* and *untrustworthy* then I simply get rid of him.—What's the problem?'

Vera lowered her head. She wanted to cry, she wanted run away and never stop running. Her head was spinning and she could smell *Daddy's* vile breath and feel him probing her. *Is this really happening to me? Will I wake up any moment now from this nightmare?*

A nightmare, in fact, that started when Jessica was a child. Just day's after her half-brother, Roger Boardman, was born, *his* father, 'Daddy,' left home. A year later their mother met another man, named Stan Whatley, and they had Jessica and her younger brother, Sean, together. Stan was a loving father to Jessica but he was tragically killed in a crane accident on the docks when Jessica was just six-years-old.

Soon after Stan's death, 'Daddy' moved back into the house on Mellish Street and Jessica's happy childhood came to an *abrupt* end.

Weldon continued. 'He was quite honest with me Vera, he said he had no intention of going back to London. In fact he said to me: 'This job is going to be the making of me, Doctor. You won't regret taking me on, I can assure you of that.' And when I eventually offered him the job he shook my hand so hard I thought he was going to break my bloody fingers!'

Weldon settled on the edge of Vera's bed and slipped his hand up her shirt.

'*Don't* touch me Tony! I'm really not in the mood.'

'That's okay, I understand... I promised to drive Phillip to the pub tonight for a couple of pints so I'll leave you to it. It'll help him to get settled into the place. I don't suppose you want to join us?'

'No, I don't!' Vera answered, emphatically.

'Okay—calm down. Take some aspirin and have an early night. Hopefully you'll feel better in the morning.'

Somehow I don't think so, she thought.

When Weldon left her alone in her room, Vera broke down on the bed, sobbing uncontrollably.

'He's come for me,' she said. 'I bloody knew he would.'

Roger Boardman had been shown to his one-room apartment on the top floor of the main building by a rather nervous and chatty Nurse Griffith, who'd wished him well in his new job, before leaving him alone in his room.

He was lying on his single bed smoking a cigarette and still trembling with excitement at being offered the job of Junior Clinical Psychologist. His confidence, self-belief, innate intelligence and weeks of studious research in libraries had paid off—but only just. A number of times during the interview with Weldon he felt uneasy and out of his depth, but Weldon was very forgiving and easy going, which helped Manson to relax and focus.

As he blew smoke rings towards the ceiling he remembered Jessica's horror-struck face, the moment she'd realised it was *him*—her half-brother. The one she despised.

They'd hated each other for as long as he could remember but after she'd killed *Daddy* he vowed to revenge his death. And now God had worked his magic and brought Jessica to him to face her punishment.

Boardman repeated Jessica's words in a mocking tone: 'I'm afraid you're mistaken, sir, my name is Vera Parsons'… *Vera fucking Parsons? So, Jessica Whatley is now Nurse Vera Parsons and me, Roger Boardman, well, I'm now Clinical Psychologist Phillip Manson— who'd have thought that, Daddy? …I need to get to her.*

I need to make sure she keeps her fucking mouth shut, the murderous little bitch. She must realise that if she says one bad word about me then I'll make sure she hangs for murdering Daddy.

Manson donned an insipid grin and his cheeks imploded as he pulled on his cigarette. 'This is just the start of my new life—and I ain't gonna let that little feckin cow get in my way,' he mouthed quietly to himself.

After a struggle he eventually managed to open the only window in the room; he leaned out and cleared his lungs of smoke before flicking his glowing cigarette-end into the air. Below him, some fifty yards away, swans glided effortlessly on the glassy lake; but the view never registered with him, he was deep in thought.

It would be a real shame if I had to slit the little cunt's throat, he mused and began to snigger.

He then turned the key in the door lock and pulled the handle to make sure it was locked before opening his suitcase. Under some folded shirts he found the large brown envelope and tipped its contents onto the bed cover. About thirty black and white photographs fell out. He picked one of them up and looked at it.

'You *dirty* little bitch,' he said, to himself, and with trembling hands he struggled to unbuttoned his flies.

Chapter 24

I would crawl happy from her love bed

Cornish returned to his office with two cups of coffee. 'We've made progress today, Melanie.'

'Yes, we have; at least we now know they're related and why Vera did what she did.'

Cornish pensively touched his fingertips together again. 'Let's not jump too far ahead of ourselves... Vera's a crafty old fox you know. She's feeding us information like we're fish in a tank. Vera is telling us just what *she* wants us to know, and nothing more.'

'Yes, I agree with you, she is a very manipulative lady. But I can understand why she didn't want her brother to *hang* and by remaining silent for ten years she achieved her objective; he got away with it. Blood is thicker than water, as they say.'

Cornish asked: 'But why is she holding back on who *she* really is? Her brother's dead now so I can only assume she's protecting...'

'Herself,' Melanie interjected.

'Exactly! So what is she hiding from us? We don't think she killed Weldon, so it can't be that, can it?'

'Maybe she's simply enjoying the attention and *playing* with us?' Melanie suggested.

'That's highly possible,' Cornish agreed. 'There's something bugging me though, Melanie; something about her and her brother, if he is her brother, because I'm not yet convinced he is, even though she admitted it. Firstly he was brutally murdered but she never talks about it, or why he was murdered. It's as if he meant nothing to her.'

'Are you suggesting she killed her own brother; the brother she *loved with all her heart*?'

'No, I'm not. But there's more to this enigma than meets the eye; and it's beginning to fascinate me.' Cornish walked around the office assimilating the evidence and sipping his coffee.

'Alan—what if Vera's brother had something on her and she stayed silent not to protect her brother, but to protect *herself*?'

Cornish stopped walking around. 'You mean Manson killed Doctor Weldon, for whatever reason,

152

knowing Vera would take the wrap for it, because if she didn't he would expose her for some other—'

'What if our Vera was a murderer *too*?' Melanie interjected, 'It's a possibility isn't it? Although I must admit it's hard to imagine now. Maybe he knew something about her that could've sent *her* to the gallows?'

'So he could kill Weldon knowing she'd stay silent and take the blame for him and by staying silent, literally, avoid the hangman's noose? You're suggesting some kind of weird family blackmail thing aren't you?'

'Yes, I am.'

'… The more you think about this case the more intriguing it gets.'

Cornish checked his watch. 'Christ! Look at the time… Do you fancy a drink?'

Melanie glanced at her watch. 'Well, I was expecting to go out tonight with a friend, but he hasn't called me to confirm it.'

'Oh,' was all Cornish could manage at the mention of the word *he*. 'Some other time perhaps?'

'No…tonight is fine. I'd be happy to join you for a drink.'

'I don't want to cause any problems between you and your friend,' Cornish added.

'You won't,' Melanie said, standing up. 'To be honest I'm quite relieved—campanology is not really my scene.'

'Bell-ringing?' exclaimed Cornish.

'Yes, I know. He's a friend of my Father's and my Father, bless him, suggested to him that I might like to join his bell ringer's society. I can hear my father now: "Good character building stuff Walter, It'll do her the world-of-good to get out and meet people."'

'So Walter didn't get back to you then?'

'No, he didn't, but he is *eighty-six!* He probably forgot!'

Cornish laughed and his sudden anxiety melted away. 'This might surprise you Melanie but I can't imaging you as a bell ringer.'

'I know—but Walter is such a lovely man I just couldn't refuse him when he called me up... I hope he's okay.'

'Do you want to call him?'

'No, not now—just in case.'

'In case of what?'

'In case I miss out on the drink from *you* because it doesn't happen very often!'

Cornish shook his head and smiled. 'Well, you'd better make the most of it then,' he said.

Melanie moved so close to Cornish he could feel her breath on his face when she whispered, 'I intend to, Mister Cornish.' With that she turned and strode confidently out of the office.

Cornish slumped into his chair. 'Is this *really* happening to me?' he asked himself.

He was scared to make a move that might frighten her off; he couldn't bear that, so he'd decided that *she* must be the one to make all the moves, if that's what *she* really wanted. He knew it was breaking all the rules but he couldn't stop himself. He swore never to get involved with anyone at work. He knew it was unprofessional and would only lead to problems, but Melanie's personality and beauty had dismantled his once inviolable work ethic.

If she wanted him, he knew that he wouldn't be able to resist her.

I would crawl happy from her love bed.

Chapter 25

It was such a hideous crime

Melanie was chatting to Zeezee about his passion for Harley Davidson's and how he was about to buy his third bike when Cornish joined them in the kitchenette looking very pleased with himself.

'I have some very exciting news guys,' he said, pressing the latte button on the coffee machine and waiting for his cup to fill.

'Well, what is it?' Melanie asked, impatiently.

'I've been talking to DCI Collier at Yorkshire Police's Serious Crimes Unit regarding Phillip Manson's case. At the time of the murder in 1970 the investigation was being run by a Detective Superintendent Blackburn and because of the hideous nature of the crime he, in his infinite wisdom, Blackburn that is, decided to freeze samples from the scene of the crime for possible future use. Believe it or believe it not they still have those samples.'

'Wow!' exclaimed Zeezee.

'Are they prepared to release them?' Melanie asked.

Cornish nodded. 'Yes, they are. They were aware of us from our success with the Waterstone and Mackelworth cases, and the current SIO was quite happy for us to uncover any new evidence that might allow them, or us, to solve the case and possibly get a conviction. As a matter of fact I've already arranged for the samples to be shipped to Copeland and Associates for forensic testing. I'm seeing Christoper Copeland this afternoon to discuss the implications.'

'Who's Christoper Copeland?' Melanie asked.

'Oh, of course—you haven't met him yet, have you? Christoper is the founder of Copeland and Associates and a genius when it comes to forensics. It might be a good idea if you come with me to meet him. He's a very useful contact indeed.'

'What time is the meeting?'

'One-forty-five. Actually it's a lunch meeting at the Old Bridge Hotel in Huntington, straight up the A14. It's his favourite place to eat.'

Melanie frowned. 'Are you sure you want to drag me along? I've got plenty of work to carry on with.'

'Actually Melanie, you'll find it extremely informative; the man's a genius,' Zeezee added.

When Cornish and Melanie arrived at the Old Bridge Hotel Melanie was struck by the unique character of the place. The hotel, next to the River Great Ouse, was covered in greenery with just the hotel's name, in big gold letters, and its panelled windows escaping the leafy cladding. The place looked to Melanie as if it was a living entity rather than just bricks and mortar.

It's like a creature from a Harry Potter movie, she thought. *Any minute now it's going to move.*

They were shown to the terrace near the river where Christopher Copeland was sitting, enjoying a pint of real ale. When he saw them approach he got to his feet and held out his hand.

'Great to see you again Alan,' he said.

Cornish shook his hand. 'Great to see you, mate. Christoper, this is my colleague, Melanie Underwood.'

Melanie walked forward and shook his hand.

'Lovely to meet you Melanie,' Copeland said. 'You must be new to Alan's organisation?'

'Yes, I am the latest recruit.'

'Melanie is specialising in criminal psychology, Cornish explained. She's doing her PhD on it.'

'Best of luck with that Melanie. I could never get my head around psychology,' Copeland said.

Cornish cringed. 'Your jokes do not get any better, Christopher.'

Copeland chuckled and gestured for them to sit at the table. 'Pint Alan?' he asked.

Cornish glanced at Melanie and she smiled and nodded knowingly.

'Doom Bar, please,' he said, jovially.

'And what can I get you young lady?'

'A black coffee would be lovely, thank you.'

Copeland asked a passing waitress for three menus and ordered the drinks at the same time.

Melanie took an instant liking to Copeland, not only was he, according to Zeezee, a genius, but he also looked like one with his Albert Einstein wiry fly-away hair. Melanie estimated his age to be around fifty. He wore round, gold-rimmed glasses that reminded her of John Lennon, an open-necked denim shirt, cream coloured chinos and moccasins.

'You must bring Melanie to our place at some point Alan.'

'Could she come when you do the tests?' Cornish asked.

'I don't see why not. Talking of tests I think you need to fill me in on what's going on, don't you?'

Cornish glanced at Melanie. 'Would you like to give Christoper a quick overview of the situation?'

Melanie waited until the waiter had finished serving their drinks before she started speaking:

'We are currently investigating two murders. One that happened in 1952 in a secure mental hospital in Wales and another particularly *brutal* murder that happened in York, in 1970. Both murders are still unsolved. We believe that the murders are related and involve a man and a woman who are possibly brother and sister. The brother is dead; he was actually the York victim, but the woman is still alive and in fact you recently did a DNA test on her for us.'

'Yes, I remember that,' Copeland said, 'her cigarette butt.'

Melanie continued. 'You'll soon receive more material for DNA testing from Yorkshire Police, taken from the scene of the murder.'

'They've kept the evidence on ice all of this time,' Cornish added.

Copeland raised his eyebrows. 'Now that is a stroke of luck.'

Melanie continued. 'What we want to know is, are they actually brother and sister.'

'Have you tried asking this woman?' Copeland enquired. 'I mean, she's still alive, right?'

Melanie sipped her coffee before answering:

'…Yes, we have, but this woman is rather complex. Getting honest answers out of her is not that easy. She's playing a *game* with us and enjoying every minute.'

'That's why I prefer forensics; it's much more black and white.'

Melanie nodded in agreement. 'So, Christopher, if you have both sets of DNA to compare, what can you tell us about our suspects?'

Chapter 26

They might be brother and sister

'Quite a lot actually, Melanie,' Copeland answered, enthusiastically, 'because DNA is bloody *magical.* I presume you guys have a basic understanding of this stuff, like, DNA is a double-helix structure with four nitrogen bases: A, C, T and G? It's the *carrier* of our *genetic* information via our genes. Codes in fact, telling our bodies what proteins to make.'

Cornish and Melanie looked bemused.

'Don't worry—you don't really need to know *any* of that stuff. All you need to know is that each parent contributes fifty percent of their DNA to their offspring. So *your* DNA, Melanie, is made up of half from your *father* and half from your *mother.*'

Melanie smiled and nodded.

'Now, Melanie, let's just *pretend* you have a child with Alan.'

Cornish smirked, tight-lipped, at Copeland.

Copeland smiled and continued. 'Your child will inherit *half* of your DNA and *half* of Alan's. Consequently when *your* child has children of its own your grandchildren will inherit a *quarter* of *each* of your DNA codes. Clever stuff isn't it? Do you follow?'

Cornish and Melanie nodded slowly.

Melanie said:

'So our DNA code is halved in each successive generation?'

'Exactly, Melanie,' Copeland continued, 'if the DNA tests are successful we will be able to tell you if these two people are related or not, as the case may be. They might be brother and sister—or—it's possible that they are half-brother and sister, where they share only one parent and only *twenty-five-percent* of that particular parent's DNA. There are some other possible combinations like grandfather and granddaughter, aunt and nephew or double cousins, but, let's not get bogged down with the *less* likely combinations at this stage of the tests.'

Cornish asked:

'Shall we order some lunch?'

'Great idea!' exclaimed Copeland.

'Yes, great idea,' Melanie agreed.

Forty minutes later the trio had finished eating and were enjoying coffee and mints.

Melanie had found the conversation over lunch enthralling; listening intently to Copeland describing his efforts to set up Copeland and Associates some twenty-years-ago.

Cornish had a similar story to tell about the setting up of Probe.

Having listened to their start-up stories, Melanie felt an even greater admiration for the two men sitting next to her. She now realised that both their companies had struggled in the early days but now, both companies were *flourishing,* thanks to police outsourcing due to diminishing police budgets and alarming increases in the crime rate. But far more importantly their success was based on their *highly* professional services with excellent reputations, built up over many years.

'When do you think you'll have the results, Christopher?' Cornish asked.

'When do we got our hands on the samples?'

'Tomorrow—by courier,' responded Cornish.

'Well, it all depends.'

'On what?'

'On the *condition* and the *nature* of the samples we have to work with, but far more importantly it depends on whether *you* buy lunch or not my boy!'

'Well, we know the answer to that one don't we?' Cornish smirked before finishing his coffee.

'As soon as we have some results I will call you.'

Cornish smiled. 'We look forward to it, Christopher.'

'Melanie, it's been a real pleasure to meet you, my dear. Call my secretary tomorrow if you want to visit us during the tests and she'll arrange everything. Our offices are only down the road in St. Ives. You'll be more than welcome to see how we deal with our biggest enemy.'

Melanie frowned. 'Enemy?'

'*Contamination*, young lady; especially if there's a conviction based on the results. Prepare to be suited-and-booted as they say.'

Melanie and Christoper stood up and shook hands again.

'Thank you, I really appreciate your kind offer,' she said. 'It all sounds rather exciting.'

Chapter 27

Vera, I need a word in your ear

(Llanarth Court, 1952)

It was now just over a week since Vera's world had fallen apart. She had seen very little of Weldon, as he'd spent most of his time with the 'new boy,' Phillip Manson. Thankfully she had not seen Him at all, other than brief glimpses of him as he walked around with Weldon like he owned the fucking place.

Tomorrow was Saturday and she was looking forward to a picnic with Tony on the top of the Holy Mountain, as he called it. She wasn't sure where it was and it really didn't matter that much anyway. What really mattered was that she would have Weldon all to herself. There were things she needed to say and they needed to be said in private.

Vera walked into the canteen to have a quick lunch and after queuing for some bangers and mash and apple crumble she found a seat on one of the quieter tables and settled down to eat her meal. A few moments later she was approached by another nurse carrying a tray of food.

'Vera, do you mind if I join you? ...It's just that I need a word in your ear,' she said, quietly.

'Sit down Jane. What's it all about?'

Nurse Jane Harris was a pretty twenty-year-old with curly fair hair, ruddy complexion and large bosoms that made her very popular with the male staff and patients alike. She sat down next to Vera and looked around nervously.

'...I understand that you and Doctor Weldon are now a—*proper* couple. Is that true?'

Vera looked confused. '...Yeah—but what if we are?'

'Well, it's just that I think you should be aware of something.'

'Go on,' Vera said, intrigued.

'...My sister knows someone who used to work with him in Manchester. He was a doctor on the children's wards up there. He didn't go to war like most of our boys, he stayed behind.'

Vera's heart began to race as Tony's explicit war stories came to mind.

Nurse Harris continued:

'This friend of my sister's told her that he had been reported on a number of occasions for, allegedly,' the nurse moved closer to Vera and mouthed quietly, 'touching-up his patients.'

Vera dropped her knife and fork on the plate.

'Apparently he was found not guilty at the tribunal but he was asked to leave the hospital. I'm sorry if it's upset you Vera, but I thought it only right that you should know... You might be going out with a paedophile?'

Vera's eyes filled with tears as she sat in stunned silence; her whole body was trembling like a volcano building up to a cataclysmic eruption.

Chapter 28

I've never done it in the open air before

(Skirrid Fawr, Monmouthshire, 1952)

The sky was a beautiful azure blue and the gentle breeze blowing from the south was warm and exhilarating; a rare day indeed on the Skirrid Fawr. Today, the views from the top of the 'Holy Mountain' were magnificent; a reward for their one-hour's hard climb through young deciduous woodland and up the steep well-trodden rocky path to the summit; a trek which left them both breathless.

Looking south, Vera could see the Bristol Channel and to the west, the rugged Black Mountains looked formidable, even under the warm summer sun. Below, to the south-west, the market town of Abergavenny and the winding River Usk were visible, nestled in the lee of the Blorenge Hill. To the north, with the aid of

Weldon's binoculars, Vera could just make out the hazy, shimmering form of Hereford Cathedral.

'Do you realise Vera, you're actually one-thousand-five-hundred-and-ninety-four-feet above sea level?'

'Plus the height of this stone, which must be at least another four feet,' she replied, as she peered through the binoculars like a soldier on look-out duty.

'It's the Skirrid Fawr or Holy Mountain as the locals call it,' Weldon said, studying his map and lighting a cigarette as he stood next to the ordnance survey point. 'There's supposed to be the remains of a Saint Michael's chapel up here somewhere but I'm buggered if I can find any evidence of it. And that side of the mountain over there,' Weldon pointed down the northwest-side, 'that supposedly broke away in a violent earthquake the precise moment Jesus Christ was nailed to the cross—if you believe all that religious tosh of course.'

'Who in their right mind would build a chapel up here?' Vera asked herself, not really listening to Weldon's chatter. She focused the binoculars on a steam-train far below as it trundled past, heading north, leaving in its wake a long plume of white smoke and steam that resembled a distant feather floating gently on the breeze.

'Come and sit down darling, I've got some lovely fresh bread and Welsh cheese in the basket and some local beer too.'

'I've lost my appetite to be honest Tony,' she said, carefully sliding down from the ordnance stone.

'There's something the matter isn't there? You haven't been right for some time now, have you?'

Vera sat down on the grass next to Weldon and lit a cigarette, refusing to make eye contact.

'Fancy making love up here?' he asked in eager anticipation. 'There's nobody else around for miles. I've never done it in the open air before. Come on— Let's do it!'

'Don't touch me!—Don't even come near me.'

'For God's sake what's wrong with you? I couldn't have fought you off a few weeks ago—not that I would've wanted to of course... All you wanted was my cock inside you. "Never stop fucking me Tony. I want you inside me, every minute of every day."— Remember?'

Vera looked away. 'I'm not in the mood for sex with you—okay?'

'So what exactly are you in the mood for, with me? Are you in the mood for telling me what's wrong with you?'

Vera turned to look at Weldon. '…Are you in the mood for telling me the truth?…Because, Tony, I can see for miles up here, but I can't see the real Tony Weldon who's sitting just two-feet-away! I think it's about time you were honest with me, don't you?'

Chapter 29

That experience nearly destroyed me

'What the hell are you talking about Vera?'

The tip of Vera's cigarette glowed as she inhaled.

'You were never in the bloody war were you, Tony?'

Weldon fell silent, clearly shocked by Vera's question. After some time he swallowed hard and said, weakly:

'…No.'

'So why did you lie to me?'

Weldon smiled, glanced up and took a deep breath through his nostrils as if looking for some divine intervention. Then he gazed down into Vera's eyes and said:

'…I wanted to *impress* you. I wanted you to think of me as *your* brave war hero. Because the truth is *far* less interesting. The fact is I stayed here and practiced medicine in Manchester, because I was deemed *unfit* to fight. Epilepsy I'm afraid; not serious, thanks to barbiturates, but enough to stop me going to war.'

Vera jabbed her cigarette into the grass. 'Tell me why you left Manchester?'

Weldon took a deep breath. '…I had a problem… I had to leave.'

'…What *sort* of problem, Tony?'

'…I was a doctor on the children's wards at the infirmary and there were a couple of young girl patients, fourteen or fifteen, no more. They made up this story that I was *touching-them-up*! I denied it of course, but the two girls fabricated the story between them that I couldn't disprove; even though there was no *evidence* or witnesses to back up their allegations. It was simply *their* word against *mine*. The pair of them were out to make trouble... After the tribunal, that found me *innocent of all allegations*, I was asked to leave. The incident *nearly* destroyed me.'

Vera swallowed hard as she gazed at Tony's pitiful expression. He slowly lowered his head in shame and said:

'I'm *really* sorry Vera, I should have been honest with you—but I was frightened I'd lose the best thing that has ever happened to me.'

Vera reached out and took his hand.

174

'How did you find out about me?' he asked.

'Jane told me. Her sister knows someone who worked with you in Manchester.'

Weldon looked up and smiled at Vera. 'It's a small world isn't it?' he said, pensively.

'And sometimes it's a very cruel one *too* Tony,' Vera added as she leaned over and kissed him on the lips. 'I've never done it in the open air either,' she whispered, sensuously.

Chapter 30

Your two suspects are definitely not brother and sister.

(Copeland and Associates, Huntington)

Christopher Copeland looked at Melanie and smiled. 'See that?' he said, pointing to the computer screen and the rows of boxed numbers stretching across the display. 'This is what we call the genetic fingerprint and this result shows that they share twenty-five percent of their DNA; in other words your two suspects are definitely not brother and sister.'

Melanie smiled. 'But they are *definitely* half-brother and sister.'

'Correct! The test confirms that they are half-brother and sister.'

'So—Alan is right— they are related. They share one parent,' Melanie added.

Copeland nodded in agreement. 'Precisely! But if you think that's of interest take a look at this.' Copeland selected another screen box and clicked on it. 'This is the result we got from a single hair taken from the murder scene.'

Melanie looked at the two displays of dark dashes, one above the other, but it meant nothing to her.

Copeland looked at her and smiled. 'This is a perfect match for the DNA sample you gave me.'

'You mean Vera's cigarette butt?'

'Yep, Copeland said, smiling smugly.'

'Does that mean Vera was at the scene of the crime in York?' Melanie asked excitedly?

'I'm afraid not; at least not in the eyes of the law. It simply means one of Vera's hairs was found at the scene of the crime; that's all. It could have been brought in by Manson or someone else.'

'…She did it. She killed her brother.'

'If we'd found her fingerprints or her blood at the scene of the crime then you'd have a case against her; but a single hair is not enough to convict her, I'm afraid. Just out of interest, Melanie, what did her half-brother do to get himself killed?'

'It's very simple—Doctor Weldon was the only man that Vera ever loved, and her half-brother killed him because Weldon found out that Manson's qualifications were fake and Weldon was about to expose him—I'm convinced of it.'

Copeland raised his eyebrows. 'Seems like murder runs in their family.'

Melanie nodded. 'It's beginning to look a lot like that isn't it?' After a short pause, Melanie continued:

'Vera planned everything. She avoided the noose and eventually she got her revenge on her brother.'

Copeland asked:

'But how do you intend to prove it my dear? Because it's nothing more than pure speculation at this moment in time.'

Melanie smiled. 'At this moment in time, I have no idea Christopher.'

'Getting a confession out of an eighty-five-year-old woman who was previously considered insane is not an option the courts would even consider.'

'Yes, I realise that,' Melanie replied, thoughtfully.

Chapter 31

'Yeah…that's exactly how she managed it.'

(Probe's Offices, Cambridge)

'**Well! well! well!**—Our Vera's not disappointing us, is she?' Cornish exclaimed when Melanie explained Christopher Copeland's findings to him.

Cornish stood up, picked up his glass of water and walked around the office. '…I think our theory is beginning to prove right. Vera eventually got revenge on her half-brother for killing Weldon. The only problem is,' Cornish sipped his water and smiled at Melanie through tight lips, 'we don't have a scrap of proof.'

'Yes, I realise that. Christopher explained to me that finding her hair there doesn't prove she was actually at the scene of the murder.' Melanie fell silent, deep in thought; eventually she said:

'...So the bullshit she fed us about her loving brother is just another one of her fabricated lies!'

'Mmmm,' Cornish replied, pensively. 'It makes me wonder if she's actually capable of telling the truth at all?'

'She loved Weldon, I'm sure of that, Alan.'

Cornish nodded. 'You're probably right and I must admit I do find it hard to believe that Vera Parsons was capable of doing that.' Cornish pointed to the photos of the murder scene on the cork board.

'But you only know her as a frail old woman, Alan. When that happened she was in the prime of her life'

'Yeah, that's true. So how did she manage to hang Manson upside down and push a knife into his head so hard it broke through the top of his skull?'

'...My guess is she drugged him? After all she was a trained nurse with a knowledge of tranquillisers.'

Cornish nodded, knowingly. '...Yes—that's exactly how she managed it,' he said, as another piece of his mental jigsaw fell into place; augmenting his nascent theories.

Cornish pondered for a moment and then said:

'I wonder if Christopher has enough of Manson's blood to test for antipsychotics or CNS depressants?'

Melanie stood up and walked over to the gruesome black and white photos of Manson's mutilated body that were pinned to the cork-board behind Cornish.

'Looking at these,' she said, 'I'd say there was definitely no shortage of his blood for samples. It's like a scene from a slaughterhouse... This is the work of an experienced cold-blooded killer.'

'I would suggest serial killer. But why did she cut off his genitals?'

Melanie thought about it for a moment. '...She was making a statement because—'

Cornish finished her sentence:

'She'd been sexually abused by him.'

'Exactly! Her *loving* brother.'

'Yeah, the brother that meant the world to her; the man that killed her lover and sexually abused her— Christ! It's no wonder she's screwed up. I wonder how many other people she's killed?' Cornish picked up the phone and speed-dialled Copeland and Associates.

'Jesus! I've really kicked a hornet's nest this time, Alan.'

Cornish smiled and nodded. 'Plenty to talk about over a cold beer and a curry!'

Melanie smiled and nodded. *I'm beginning to love this job.*

Chapter 32

Why did you kill him?

(Llanarth Court 1952)

When Vera arrived at the canteen it was deserted. She checked her watch as she walked up to the serving counter.

'You're late Vera,' came a voice from behind the serving counter.

'Edna, any chance of something to eat, love?'

'Oh, I'm sure we can find something for you, sweetheart.'

'You are a darling, Edna,' Vera said, grinning.

'…I've got some cottage pie left over and I've got some pork chops as well.'

'Ohhhh, I think I'll have a pork chop please.'

'Cabbage mash and gravy, my love?'

'Oh yes please!'

'Some rice pudding to finish?'

'You are a treasure. Can I have some skin if there's any left?'

'You're in luck,' Edna said, serving up the food onto plates on the counter. 'My old man will just have to go without. He's a bugger for the skin too.'

'Thank you so much. I didn't think I'd get any lunch at one point. One of our patients had a fit this morning and it took three of us to get her under control. She threatened to kill Doctor Weldon.'

'Oh dear,' said Edna.

'She's calmed down now; these new tranquilliser drugs are a bloody godsend.'

'Thank heavens for that,' Edna said. 'Enjoy your meal, my darling.'

'I intend to,' Vera called out as she walked to a table with her tray of food.

Moments later a familiar voice from behind her said:

'Well, well, if it isn't my little sister.'

Vera looked around to see Manson standing there.

In a quiet voice she asked:

'What do you want? Why did you come looking for me?'

'Don't flatter yourself, Jess! I don't give a *fuck* about you,' he said, settling onto a chair opposite her at the table and lighting a cigarette.

'It's Vera. My name's Vera!'

Manson smirked. '...I didn't come here looking for *you*. I came here to make a new life for *myself*.'

Vera fell silent for a moment, digesting Manson's words. 'How's Muvver?' she eventually asked.

'As if you feckin care!'

'...How is she?'

'The last time I saw her she was drinking and smoking herself into an early grave; so, no change really.'

'How's my brother and the baby?' Vera asked.

Manson didn't answer.

'I said how's my—'

'Sean's dead—and the baby was taken into care.'

Vera struggled to catch her breath and tears filled her eyes.

Manson continued. 'As usual, Sean was playing somewhere where he shouldn't 'ave—and a bomb exploded. It killed him, the Conway twins and little Charlie Thomas as well.'

'Oh my God!'

'They took the baby away from us the day after you cooked Daddy's brains.'

Vera wiped tears from her eyes with her fingers.

Manson leaned forward, stony faced. 'Why did you kill him?'

Vera swallowed hard and took a deep breath. 'You know why.'

'Tell me why?'

'…Because he was a dirty fucking *pervert*, that's why.'

Manson breathed in through bared teeth. 'I can still smell the stench of his burnt flesh.'

Vera was trembling. 'He was a fucking *monster!* He abused me nearly every day. He made me do things to him; disgusting things… I was just a *child*!'

'What sort of fings?' Manson asked with a sickly tight-lipped smile.

Vera recoiled in horror.' You disgusting *pig*!'

He placed his hands on the table, leaned forward and asked:

'Did yer *moan* with pleasure when he licked yer cunt, yer dirty little whore?'

Vera's chest heaved from the anger raging inside her. 'That evil monster lives on in YOU!' she yelled, in disbelief and lurched forward, stabbing her fork deep into Manson's hand.

Manson's face contorted and drained of blood as he looked down in disbelief at his hand.

'*You fucking cow*!' he shrieked, grimacing, as he struggled to pull the fork out of his hand.

Vera picked up her knife and waved it near his neck. 'If you ever come near me again I'll gouge *your* fucking eyes out too!'

Manson winced and replied weakly:

'I do believe gouging people's eyes out is a *speciality* of yours, Jess!'

He stood up and staggered off clutching his hand and swearing revenge for what she'd done to him.

Edna was standing behind the counter with her mouth wide open.

'You didn't see that did you Edna?'

Edna swallowed hard and replied nervously:

'…See what, my love?'

Vera's eyes rolled upwards as she inhaled through her nostrils. A feeling of euphoria surged through her body.

'Cup of char, sweetheart?'

'Make it a strong one please, Edna.'

'A strong one coming up, Vera.'

Chapter 33

There's another side to her

Melanie placed the menu on the table in front of her. 'I've decided,' she said, smiling at Cornish.

'What are you having? he asked'

'I'm having a King Prawn Dhansak with coconut rice, she said.'

'Coconut rice!' I've not tried that.

'You can try some of mine. What are you having Alan?'

Cornish placed his menu down on the table. 'I'm having a Lamb Pathia and Keema Rice,' he said, emphatically, before taking a sip of his lager.

The waiter arrived and Cornish placed their order while Melanie nibbled a popadom thinking about her new plan.

When they were alone again Melanie said:

'Alan, I've got an idea.'

'Let's hear it,' he said, brightly.

'I think we should take Vera out for a few hours. You know, tea and cakes by the river, that sort of thing. We need to break down *her* barriers in the hope that she'll tell us something more about who she *really* is. She's obviously very intelligent and *very complex*. The only side of her she presents to *us* is Vera. There's another side to her though, possibly a much darker side that she's hiding from us and we need to try to get her to talk about it.'

Cornish nodded. 'How do you intend to do that?'

Melanie smiled. 'It won't be easy, but firstly we need to gain her trust. She needs to feel comfortable with us and not apprehensive. When we take her out we initially won't ask her any personal questions.'

Cornish frowned. 'So how's that going to work?'

'It'll give her time to relax. We *need* her to feel relaxed in our company. In that state of mind she might become talkative and more receptive to *carefully* worded questions. If you and I talk casually about *our* childhood experiences over tea and cakes that might be the *catalyst* to get Vera talking about her childhood. I call them memory moments. It's a long shot, but it's the only idea I can come up with right now.'

'Well, it's worth a try. Anything she tells us at this stage of the investigation is a bonus, so long as it's the *truth*.'

Two days later

Melanie walked arm-in-arm with Vera onto the sun terrace that overlooked the River Cam. The sun was shining and the river was busy with tourists enjoying the warm sunshine. Swans moved gracefully on the water, deftly avoiding the tourist laden punts that passed by.

'Where would you like to sit Vera?' Melanie asked.

'Over there, in the shade, overlooking the river; that would be nice, my dear... Is your man not joining us then?'

'Yes, he is, but he had to take a call. He'll be here soon.' As she said that Cornish walked out onto the terrace.

Vera saw him and waved. 'Over here handsome,' she called out. 'It's so peaceful here isn't it? I love swans,' she added in the same breath.

'I've got the menu,' Cornish said, 'but I'm going for the afternoon tea and scones option.'

Vera raised her eyebrows. 'I'm going to have the same; it's years since I had afternoon tea and scones.'

'We'll have three lots of tea and scones, please,' Melanie said, as a waitress arrived.

'Jam and clotted cream?' the young girl asked.

'Ohhhh, yes please,' Vera said, excitedly.

'Shall I bring you a large pot of tea for three?'

'Can we have loose-leaf tea, please?' Melanie asked.

'We have Assam or English Breakfast.'

'English Breakfast will do nicely.'

Vera looked very summery in her floral dress and broad-rimmed summer hat. She giggled as she waved to a passing punt, full of camera wielding Japanese tourists, who waved back excitedly.

'It's lovely here,' Vera said. 'I could sit here all day watching the river.' Another punt passed by and Vera waved enthusiastically to the smiling passengers who dutifully waved back.

Cornish glanced at Melanie and she smiled at him.

So-far-so-good, she thought.

'Here comes our afternoon teas,' he said as a waitress approached their table carrying a large tray.

Vera rubbed her hands together. 'I'm really looking forward to this,' she said, excitedly, as the waitress placed the tea and scones on the table.

'So are you two an item now?' Vera asked, bluntly.

Cornish smiled and looked at Melanie who blushed with embarrassment.

'…No, Vera we're not an item, as such,' Melanie responded.

'Why on earth not, you're both in love with each other, aren't you? It's bloody obvious.'

Chapter 34

I mean nobody ever bloody asked me

'What's the matter with you handsome, no lead in your pencil?' Vera asked. 'Give the girl a good seeing to.'

Cornish managed a somewhat embarrassed smile and Melanie blushed again.

Vera cut a scone in half and dipped her spoon into the strawberry jam. 'Life's too short to waste; you'll only regret it if you don't.' Vera lavished her scone halves with jam and winked at Melanie. 'Pass the cream, handsome,' she said to Cornish.

Cornish obliged and glanced at Melanie who was already looking at him, warmly. He smiled at her and she smiled back.

I wonder if he'll take her advice? Melanie thought.

'Did you ever marry, Vera?' Melanie asked.

Vera shook her head. 'No, I never did get married. I'm not the marrying kind, I'm afraid.'

'What do you mean by that, Vera?' Cornish asked.

'…I mean nobody ever bloody asked me! But I'm still available if you're interested, handsome.'

Cornish laughed and said:

'Let me think about it.'

'Well, don't leave it too long, in case I get snapped up.'

Everyone laughed at Vera's witty comment, including Vera.

'Ummm—these scones are lovely,' Melanie said, 'they're almost as good as my mother's.'

'My mother was a terrible cook,' Cornish confessed.

'What about your mum, Vera, was she a good cook?'

Vera grinned. '…My dear, when I was a child, if your mother didn't cook you starved. And after the war food was scarce for a long time; but there was always food to be had around the docks, if you were *smart.*'

Cornish glance at Vera. *Docks,* he thought.

'Was that London's docks, Vera?' Melanie asked.

'…Yes—I grew up in the docklands.'

Cornish remained silent. *Nice one Melanie!*

Vera continued. 'My early memories are *really* happy ones... my father was a lovely man... Jess, he used to say to me when he came home from work, look what I've got for yer. I knew what it was of course, it was *always* a banana—except once when it was an orange. But he died in an accident on the docks when I was just six-years-old. I moved away just after the end of the war in 1946, when I was fourteen, and became a nurse, as you know.'

Melanie poured out the tea and winked at Cornish.

Zeezee took about forty minutes searching various public and private internet databases to find the answers he was looking for, using the information passed on to him by Cornish and Melanie when they returned to the office after their time spent with Vera.

Zeezee called up Cornish from his desk phone:

'Alan, I've got some answers for you,' he said.

Cornish asked Zeezee to join him in his office and to bring Melanie with him.

When they arrived Cornish was sitting at his desk talking on the phone. He gestured for them to sit at the table in the corner. A few minutes later he'd finished the phone conversation.

'Sorry about that guys,' he said, making his way to the table. 'So, tell us what you've found Zeezee?'

Zeezee opened his file and when Cornish was seated he began:

'I found the digitised dockland records of deaths on the docks for that period and a number of names came up, as you can imaging; no Health and Safety in those days. I also searched Births Deaths and Marriages for children named Jess or Jessica born in the area. I found out that a Stanley Whatley was killed on the docks in 1938. He was married to an Irish woman named Mary and they had a girl, born in 1932, named—Jessica Whatley. They lived in Mellish Street near the Millwall docks. But wait for this,' Zeezee enthused, clearly enjoying the moment, 'I've found some more information that I think might be very relevant...I *love* relational databases,' he added, with intensity in his voice. 'Jessica Whatley went *missing* in 1946, aged fourteen, and was never seen again. The very same day she went missing, her stepfather, a bloke by the name of Frank Boardman, was murdered in the living room of their house in Mellish Street with a hot poker, shoved in his eye socket!'

'Oh my God!'Melanie exclaimed.

Cornish nodded.

'So... Vera Parsons is actually Jessica Whatley and Phillip Manson is...?'

'Her half-brother, aka Roger Boardman,' Zeezee interjected, answering Melanie's question.

'Melanie, that was one bloody *awesome* idea of yours.'

Melanie smiled. 'Thank you Alan. It certainly got her to open up, didn't it? Did you notice that she only talked about her *early* life? Obviously a time when she was a normal, *happy* child. She never touched on anything that might have been too painful for her. And, I *suspect* she thought that what she was telling us wouldn't reveal to us who she really was... The person who *murdered* her stepfather?'

'Why would a fourteen-year-old girl kill her stepfather?' Zeezee asked.

'I can make an educated guess,' Cornish replied.

Melanie looked at Zeezee. 'My bet is Frank Boardman was a paedophile, sexually abusing her?'

'Yeah, my money's on that, too,' Cornish replied. 'And while I'm at it, I think I'll do the double; my money's also on Vera being a *serial-killer!*'

Melanie sighed. 'An innocent child, selfishly nurtured by her perverted stepfather into a dangerous psychopath...It's quite ironic isn't it that the monster was killed by *another* monster.'

'Very Mary Shelley,' Cornish added.

'We don't know that for sure, Melanie,' Zeezee interjected.

Cornish stood up. 'There's a *lot* we don't know, Zeezee, but we're definitely making progress. Thank you guys; that was a great day's investigative work.'

Zeezee picked up his file and headed back to his desk, leaving Cornish and Melanie alone.

'That woman is very astute, isn't she?' Cornish suggested. 'I think she got it right, too.'

Melanie said:

'I'd like to think so, *handsome.*'

'If I do leave it too long though, she'll definitely be snapped up.'

Melanie moved close to Cornish. With a wry smile she asked:

'Do you think I could *entice* you away from her with an offer of supper and a nice bottle of red wine?'

'I doubt it, I'm into serial killers. How nice is the wine?'

'It's under a tenner, from Waitrose.'

'That's my favourite!' Cornish said, trying to remain cool. 'Shall I bring a bottle as well?'

'So long as you don't intend to drive home afterwards.'

'It looks like the guest room for me then.'

'Sorry, but that's being redecorated.'

'Ohhhh,' said Cornish, leaving his mouth open.

Melanie turned and walked out of the office, biting her bottom lip. 'See you at seven-thirty?' she said, leaning around the door. 'By the way—it's filet du boeuf en croûte—rare.'

'…I'll see you at seven-thirty,' Cornish replied, in a soft, trance-like lilt. With his finger and thumb he pinched his arm. 'No, it isn't a dream, Alan,' he reminded himself.

Chapter 35

You can't win them all, Alan

(Copeland and Associates, Huntington)

Alan Cornish parked his Jaguar in the only available visitor's parking space outside the offices of Copeland and Associates and switched off the engine. It was only then that he realised he couldn't remember the drive from Melanie's apartment to here. It was as if he'd been on autopilot. His mind was fully occupied with thoughts of Melanie and the way they'd become lovers.

He could have walked away from the temptation a few weeks ago, before he really got to know her. But last night he knowingly and willingly crossed the line. Making love to her was so bloody easy, so natural, so enjoyable. She had a way of making him feel confident with himself again; something time had taken away from him. Her beauty wasn't just skin deep, she was a genuinely lovable person and Cornish had fallen in love with her long before they'd actually made passionate love on the kitchen table, the stairs and the bedroom.

It can still work, he thought. People all over the world live and work together. Why should it be a problem? She makes me feel so alive. She makes me feel young again.

A tap on the driver's window brought Cornish back to reality. He looked out to see the smiling face of Christopher Copeland peering in.

'Are you coming in or are you staying there all day?'

Cornish lowered his driver's window. 'Good morning, Christopher!'

'You look knackered Alan. What the hell have you been up to?'

Cornish chuckled. 'You'd never believe me, my friend, but it did involve some rather nice red wine.'

'French?'

'Italian—Barolo.'

'Ummm, heavy shit! I think a strong black coffee is called for then, don't you?'

'You're a bloody mind reader, Christopher.'

'How about some freshly ground *Italian* coffee?'

'Penso che sia una splendida idea!'Cornish responded as they entered the building.

Copeland's secretary arrived at his office carrying a tray of wonderfully aromatic coffee and a plate of biscuits.

'I've made a large pot of coffee,' she said, glancing at Cornish and smiling sympathetically.

'Thank you, Jane. Hobnobs or Ginger Nuts?'

'Both,' she said.

Copeland grinned and rubbed his hands together.

'This Vera Parsons case has really fired you up hasn't it, Alan?'

'Yes, it certainly has; I've never taken on anything quite like it, especially without getting paid for it,' Cornish stressed. 'It all started with Melanie's visit to see the old fox as part of her PhD research project. Melanie wanted to understand Vera's motive for killing Doctor Weldon, but what has transpired since is quite *unbelievable*. It seems that our Vera is actually a very clever serial murderer who's got away with it all these years.' Cornish sipped his coffee and felt his body respond as the caffeine kicked in.

He then continued. 'We believe that she drugged Manson before she killed him and we're hoping that you can test his blood for *proof* that he was actually drugged. We're also in contact with the police to try and find any other possible DNA matches for Vera and Manson from evidence taken from *unsolved* cases around the country; now that we know *exactly* who they are.'

'And who are they?' Copeland asked.

'They are half-brother and sister, Jessica Whatley and Roger Boardman; from the London docklands.'

'Well, once again Alan, toxicology can test his blood for drugs—and even if the tests show positive that doesn't prove it was *Vera* who administered them —unless you can come up with a syringe covered in *her* fingerprints of course.'

'Yes, I realise that. Finding *any* evidence against the wily-old-fox is proving very difficult after all this time.'

'You can't win them all, Alan.'

'I know—but this case has got under my skin and I'm determined to solve it.'

'Well, get some more of that coffee into you, you're going to need it!' Copeland said, biting into a Hobnob. 'Now, based on the time frame of this murder I would strongly suggest we test for barbiturates. It's what Llanarth would have used in the fifties and was still very common in the sixties and seventies. I would suggest it's what Vera most likely used to drug her brother in 1970.'

'How's it administered?' Cornish asked.

'Powder form normally, swallowed as a capsule. My guess is she slipped the powder into his drink. It's the same stuff that killed Marilyn Monroe.'

'I wonder if he was conscious when she cut off his tackle?' Cornish asked.

Copeland cringed. 'Even if he was conscious, it wouldn't have been for long, because looking at the evidence he basically bled to death. So he would have been unconscious in no time, what with his severed genitals and both jugular veins slashed; his *halal* death would have been pretty quick. Most definitely the workings of a *demented* mind.'

'Vera was definitely not the kind of woman to upset was she?' Cornish added.

'I think I'd rather have been hung, drawn and quartered Alan?'

Two hours later and after too much coffee, Cornish left Copeland and Associates, wide-eyed, and with the answer he was looking for. The spectral analysis of Manson's blood had tested positive for barbiturates.

'A *massive* dose,' he said to himself, repeating Copeland's words. When Cornish slipped into the driver's seat of his car he flared his nostrils and inhaled the faint scent of Melanie's unmistakable perfume: a tingle of excitement rippled down his spine like a mild electric shock. He closed his eyes and he could feel her panting breath on his face and taste the beads of perspiration on her breasts.

He was alive again.

Chapter 36

Is he a good fuck, my dear?

(Probe's Offices, Cambridge)

When Melanie walked into Cornish's office he greeted her with a broad smile.

'You look like the cat that got the cream,' she said.

'I did, I got the cream,' he replied, with a broad smile of satisfaction.

'Tell me more.'

Cornish stood up. 'Coffee?'

'Good idea!'

As they walked out of the office towards the kitchenette Cornish explained the results of Manson's blood test to Melanie.

'A massive dose?' Melanie repeated.

'Yeah—a massive dose of barbiturates. Zeezee did some more digging and discovered that the spectral analysis of the barbiturate in Manson's sample was exactly the same as the barbiturate used at Llanarth Court during Vera's time there. It looks very much like Vera planned and murdered her own half-brother.'

'Hence the lack of evidence against her,' Melanie noted.

Cornish nodded. 'Planned murders are always a nightmare for any SIO.'

'I think it's time we confronted her again, don't you?'

Cornish nodded again. 'Yes, I do. Especially as we now know exactly who she and Manson really are. And as she's now a suspect, in line with PACE 1984, she has to be cautioned before any further questioning.'

'Leave it to me,' Melanie responded as she pressed the latte button on the coffee machine.

Melanie and Cornish walked across the lawn towards the unmistakably enigmatic figure sitting on the bench.

'I'm so glad you picked a fine day,' Cornish whispered as they walked side by side. 'There's no smell of urine out here.'

'Or boiled cabbage,' Melanie added.

Vera waved to Melanie and Melanie waved back as she approached.

'I see you've brought handsome with you,' she said before lighting a cigarette.

'Hello Vera,' Cornish responded.

Vera's cheeks imploded as she inhaled. 'What words of discovery have you got for me today then?' she asked, as smoke exuded from her nose and mouth.

Melanie held out her hand but Vera ignored it.

'Sit down,' Vera said.

'How are you today, Vera?' Melanie asked.

'Well, that depends on what you've got to say, my dear.'

Melanie sensed that Vera was on edge and not her normal confident self. 'We've done some more investigating, Vera.'

'Well, that's your job isn't it?' Vera responded.

Melanie glanced briefly at Cornish. 'Vera, we now know who you are and we also know for definite who Phillip Manson was.'

'Really! So who am I then?'

'Your real name is Jessica Whatley and Phillip Manson was your half-brother, Roger Boardman. You lived in Mellish Street in London and the very day you left home your step-father was found murdered in the living room.'

Vera sucked hard on her cigarette. 'That's very good —I'm very impressed. But so what? What if I am Jessica Whatley?'

'Vera,' Cornish interjected, 'we believe you killed your step-father and your half-brother, and in accordance with official protocol we must warn you under the Police and Criminal Evidence Act of 1984, that you are now officially a *suspect* in our murder investigations.'

Vera dabbed out her cigarette on the end of the bench. 'Do you now, handsome. Can you back that up with any *actual* evidence?'

'At the time of your brother's murder he was full of barbiturates. The same kind of barbiturates that were administered by you at Llanarth Court.'

Vera smiled and nodded her head. 'That's interesting isn't it. What a coincidence!'

Cornish managed a thin smile. '…Did you kill your step-father because he was sexually abusing you, Vera?'

Vera's breathing became erratic and her eyes became watery. '…But do you have any *actual* evidence that I killed either of them?'

'No—not yet,' Cornish replied.

'Well, you'd better get your skates on; I could be dead before you solve this enigma,' Vera joked.

'Why *did* you kill them, Vera?' Melanie asked.

'…That's for you to find out, isn't it?'

'You're quite enjoying this, aren't you?' Cornish suggested.

'If *you* had to live in this soul-destroying place handsome, believe me, you'd want *something* to occupy your mind…By the way, how was your first sexual experience together? Is he a good fuck, my dear?' Vera relaxed, not expecting a response to her question and lit another cigarette. 'I do hope we can have tea and scones again soon. I really enjoyed myself that day by the river, and it's good for my memory too.'

You cunning old fox, thought Cornish.

Chapter 37

He's controlling you

(Llanarth Court 1952)

Emerald green dragonflies danced above the surface of the shimmering lake as Vera settled down on her picnic blanket at the water's edge. By her side in the wicker basket was a block of cheese, slices of honey-roast ham, bread, butter, a flagon of cloudy farmhouse cider, plates, knives and forks, wrapped in cotton napkins, and two pint glasses.

A flotilla of frenzied ducks were frantically paddling towards her, like an advancing armada as Vera tossed a handful of bread pieces into the water.

'Stop squabbling! There's enough for everyone,' she called out, as they arrived at the water's edge, before throwing another handful of bread into the now turbid water.

Weldon appeared at the top of the steps that led down onto the lakeside lawn. He was wearing a short sleeved open-necked shirt, cream cotton trousers a Panama hat and sunglasses. He called out: 'If you feed them any more they'll bloody well sink!'

'You're late,' Vera said, with a smile.

'Sorry love, I can't seem to get away from this place —even on Sundays.' He walked across the lawn and kissed Vera on the lips. 'What's for lunch, gorgeous?' he asked, removing his sun glasses and peering into the basket.

'Cider!'

'That's my girl,' he said, squeezing Vera's bottom.

'Behave yourself—walls have eyes you know.'

'Who cares? Everyone knows we're an item anyway.'

'I know, but don't think for one moment that we're making love on the lawn.'

'Spoil sport! Do you realise it's three weeks since we made love on the Holy Mountain?'

'Yes, I know. How could I forget that?'

'You fucked me as if it was your last,' Weldon said, opening the cider.

'I made love to you, Tony,' Vera said as she settled down on the blanket again.

Weldon smiled and poured some cider into a glass. 'You fucked me like a woman possessed!'

Vera giggled. 'I know,' she said, confidently, as she reached up and took a sip of Weldon's drink. 'That's a bit dry for my liking,' she said, crinkling her nose and returning the glass to Weldon, 'but it will have to do.'

Weldon tried it. 'Ummm, that's just how I like it, not too dry, not too sweet,' he said, filling his glass to the top. 'You look nice today my love, is that a new dress?'

'Last year's actually, but it's one of my summer favourites.'

Vera tapped the blanket and Weldon settled down next to her.

'It won't be long now before Manson leaves us, will it?' Vera mentioned as she cut into the block of cheese.

Weldon sipped his cider and stared straight ahead.

'Tony — I said it won't belong before—'

'Yes, I heard you, Vera.'

'Well?'

'Well—the truth is I haven't found anyone to replace him; so how can I get rid of him?'

Vera's face tightened. 'But he's incompetent, arrogant and downright rude! How can you keep him?' she asked, incredulously?

Weldon shifted uncomfortably on the blanket.

'What has he got on you, Tony?' Vera asked with frustration in her voice.

'What do you mean by that?'

'He's got something on you. He's controlling you.'

Weldon huffed. 'Rubbish!' he exclaimed, before taking a long swig of cider. He nervously wiped his mouth with the back of his hand. '…He has nothing on me Vera, why should he?' he added, adamantly. '…It's just that—since the war there aren't that many young men willing to work in a mental institution—in the back of beyond. They saw enough madness in the trenches'

'So why has Manson come here then?'

'I don't know—why don't you ask him yourself?'

Vera dropped her gaze. 'I don't talk to him—I don't like him.'

'Well, until I can find a suitable replacement I'm afraid he'll just have to do.'

'Suitable replacement! You'd be much better off without him,' Vera exclaimed.

'For God's sake Vera, keep your voice down. What have you got against him anyway? He hasn't done you any harm, has he?—Just stay out of his way.'

Vera sighed. 'Oh, don't worry, I intend to.'

Weldon nodded. 'Good—now can we please stop arguing and enjoy the picnic?'

Vera forced a smile and sipped her cider in silent contemplation, knowing that she could never reveal the truth to Weldon about her half-brother and risk exposing the truth about her own background.

After some time she asked: 'Are you going to make an honest woman of me then?'

'What?'

'Are you going to put a ring on my finger?'

'What's brought this on?' Weldon asked, somewhat surprised.

'Well, that's what couples do isn't it?' Vera suggested.

'Hell, Vera—I haven't really thought about it.'

'You're just happy to fuck me when it suits you, aren't you?'

Weldon stiffened. 'I say, that's not fair.'

'But it's true, isn't it Tony?'

Weldon retaliated. 'You make it sound very one sided. As if it's only me that's getting something out of this relationship.'

'I'm not saying that. I just want to know where I stand with you, that's all.'

Weldon looked out at the expanse of still water in silence. Eventually he turned towards Vera. 'I think a lot of you Vera,' he said, 'but I'm not sure I'm ready to commit to a serious relationship.'

Vera smiled and sipped her cider. 'So you think a lot of me do you? Does that mean I'm a good fuck?'

'Come on Vera, give me a break!'

Vera sighed and held her head in the hands. '…I'm sorry Tony, I feel on edge today; it's probably because my monthly's due any day now.'

Weldon smiled and refilled his pint glass. I'm glad to hear it, he thought, believing Vera's reason. He then lit a cigarette and stretched out on the blanket.

Vera knew the real reason for her irritable behaviour but she wasn't going to admit it to Tony. She was not sleeping well, knowing Roger was in the same building. *Why did he come here? Was he seeking revenge for the death of his father? He'd said that he didn't care about her and that his appearance at Llanarth Court was just a coincidence and that he was out to make a new life for himself, but that could've been a lie,* Vera mused. She knew that if he wanted to kill her he could—easily. He was tough, and nobody messed with him, even when he was a kid in the docklands most other kids were scared of him—cos he was hard.

When Vera was little she watched him kill a cat down by the wharf for a bet. He held it up by its back legs and hacked its head off with a knife before throwing its decapitated body into the water. It was fun, and he laughed out loud when he tossed the cat's head into Vera's face and watched her as she ran off holding her head and screaming frantically.

Phillip Manson peered out of his top-floor bedroom window at Vera and Weldon. Oh, Jessica Whatley, you cunning little fucker,—but, if you only knew the truth, he thought to himself as he flicked his cigarette butt out.

'Come back to bed, Love.'

'You want some more do you?'

'Yeah, I ain't finished with your cock yet,' said the female voice.

Manson sniggered. 'You dirty feckin whore.'

Nurse Sally Griffith pulled the bed sheets off her naked body. 'Come on, fuck me again.'

Manson swaggered back to the bed. 'Open your legs, bitch,' he said, holding his erection.

'Wait!' Sally Griffith called out, and emptied the morphine syringe into her vein. Her eyes rolled back in their sockets. '…Now fuck me,' she slurred.

Chapter 38

Does it mention the photographs?

Alan Cornish opened his eyes; next to him Melanie was sleeping peacefully. He smiled and gently caressed her cheek with his finger. 'I love you,' he whispered, before carefully slipping out from under the sheets. Two women now occupied his waking hours and often his dreams too. One woman was young and beautiful, and very unromantically described by Cornish, as a WYSIWYG: What-You-See-Is-What-You Get! Melanie was someone he'd met at a charity event over a year ago and he'd become instantly captivated with her beauty and her happy, modest disposition. Little did he realise at the time that they would become lovers, in a relationship that was now growing stronger by the day. He loved her modesty and enthusiasm for life, her *joie de vivre*! Just lying next to her seemed to recharge his batteries; it was if she had enough for both of them.

The other woman to occupy his thoughts of course was a complete contrast to Melanie. Vera Parsons was a devious and scheming old woman who enjoyed playing mind games. A murderous cunning character who was a challenge to Cornish; and more of a challenge than he cared to admit. But he was now in too deep to walk away from this fascinating enigma and he knew he needed evidence to convict her; but to date, he had none. Sometimes you need a bit of luck in this business, he thought, as he made his way to the shower.

Melanie awoke to the sound of Cornish singing in the shower.

'Someone's in a good mood,' she called out from the bed.

'Good morning, my love,' he replied. 'Vera's new signature tune,' he said. 'You can't hide your lying eyes.'

Melanie laughed. 'That woman's getting to you… Coffee, Mister Cornish?'

'Oh, go on then,' he replied.

One hour later Cornish was sitting at his desk reading the last of his fourteen emails when his phone rang. He picked up the receiver to hear the receptionist's voice say:

'Alan, I have someone on the line who wants to speak to you. He says he was the investigating officer for the Manson case, in York. His name is Bill Morrison, shall I put him through?'

'Yes please Sarah, I'd like to speak to him.'

'Putting you through.'

Cornish sat upright. 'Mister Morrison?' he said, into the mouthpiece.

'Yes, good morning Mister Cornish,' came the reply. 'My name is Bill Morrison and I was the Investigating Officer for the Manson case. I'm retired now of course but the other evening I was at a police dinner in York and I got talking to one of the officers who told me that after all these years you'd made some progress on the case—I was impressed.'

Cornish smiled. 'Good morning to you Mister Morrison.'

'Please, call me Bill.'

'Good morning, Bill. Yes, it's true—we've made some progress thanks to you for having the foresight to freeze the evidence.'

'I knew it would be useful,' he chuckled. 'They all said I was mad at the time.'

'Far from it Bill. It's allowed us to identify Manson.'

'Identify?'

'Yes. That was not his real identity. Manson's real name was Roger Boardman. He was from London and thanks to you we've linked him to his half-sister, who's currently under investigation by us for a murder that took place in 1952.'

'Good luck with that! I presume you have the case file?' Bill Morrison asked.

Cornish replied:

'Yes, we have the file, thank you.'

'Does it mention the photographs in the file?'

Cornish frowned. 'What photographs are you referring to?'

'About a year after Manson's death the terrace where he rented the house underwent major refurbishment to create a number of new luxury flats. When the floorboards were taken up in Manson's bedroom, the builders found a large selection of pornographic images. Sadly they were images of young children being sexually abused. We can't prove they were put there by Manson, but it's highly likely that Manson was a practicing paedophile and part of the ring operating in the city at the time. I just wanted to make sure you were aware of it.'

Cornish nodded. 'That is very interesting Bill. I've read Manson's file a number of times but that information isn't included in it.'

Morrison replied:

'I'm not surprised to be honest. There was a large paedophile ring in the York area at that time but I'm very sad to say it was covered up by the authorities. I was promoted that year and had no more involvement in the case. I would suggest that the photographs were destroyed and their link to Manson never made or at best forgotten about over time. I often wish I'd stayed on the case.'

'That's extremely interesting information—thank's for sharing it with us, Bill.'

'My pleasure; by-the-way, your secretary has my contact details, so feel free to call me if I can be of any further help. I'd love to see this one wrapped up, Alan.'

'Yeah, me too, Bill! You've been a great help; I'm much obliged to you.'

'As you well know Alan, sometimes what seems to be insignificant at the time can turn out to be crucial information. Goodbye and good luck.'

The call ended and Cornish replaced the receiver. 'Another piece of the jigsaw falls into place,' he said to himself with a satisfied smile and promptly tapped the speed dial button for ZeeZee.

Chapter 39

*And don't forget to include Catholic priests in your
search*

'I have just had a very interesting conversation,'
Cornish said, as ZeeZee walked into the office.

'Really, tell me more, Alan—I'm all ears.'

'I've got another parameter for your search criteria.'

'Oh good, we need all the help we can get. What is
it?'

'Paedophile.'

'Paedophile! 'repeated ZeeZee.

'Yeah, it looks like it runs in the Boardman family.'

'Who did you speak to?'

'A chap called Bill Morrison. He was the
investigating officer on the Manson case who decided
to freeze the evidence. Let's run another search based
on the London *and* York areas using it and see what it

comes up with. Include the usual associated parameters too,' Cornish added.

'Child abuse, child cruelty, sexual assault, rape?'

'Exactly—and don't forget Catholic priests in your search,' Cornish added, sternly, shaking a finger at ZeeZee.

ZeeZee chuckled. 'Now that could cause a power outage, boss!—I'm on the case,' ZeeZee said, and walked out.

Cornish called after him. 'ZeeZee, ask Melanie to come in on your way past, please.'

A moment late Melanie walked into the office. 'What's up?' she asked.

'Would it surprise you to know that, just like his father, Roger Boardman was a paedophile?—Pull up a chair.'

'How'd you know that?' Melanie asked.

'I don't yet, not for sure anyway. I had a call just now from the officer who was in charge of the Manson case, a guy named Bill Morrison; he's retired now of course.'

Melanie nodded. '…So?'

Cornish smiled. 'So—he told me that a year after Manson's death they retrieved a lot of pornographic material—children mostly, photographed being sexually abused.'

'What's that got to do with Manson?'

'They were found under the floorboards in his bedroom. It's not *definite* that they were his, but I'd bet my shirt on it. This Bill Morrison chap who called me said that, at the time, there was a known paedophile ring operating in York.'

Melanie cringed and visibly shook. 'Like father like son.'

'Quite! And it could explain why Manson went to York.'

Melanie mused in silence for a while. '…So maybe Vera killed Roger Boardman because she knew he was a pervert—just like his father?'

Cornish tapped his fingertips together. 'Vera—the *vigilante* paedophile killer!'

'I'm beginning to feel a tinge of sympathy for the old girl.'

'Funnily enough, so am I—and I never thought I'd say that about the wily old fox!'

'Alan, I'm gobsmacked to hear you say that!'

For the next hour ZeeZee tirelessly worked his magic, cross correlating various search criteria in a number of establishment and public databases, looking for anything that might be relevant to their search, but none of the results seemed of interest.

'Any luck?' Cornish asked as he approached ZeeZee's desk.

'Nothing of interest yet.'

'Don't forget the Catholic priests.'

'ZeeZee looked around at Cornish, 'I thought you were joking!'

'Not at all, I'm deadly serious.'

ZeeZee chuckled, typed in the parameters and ran another search. Twenty-seconds later he called out: 'Bingo! Sixteen results.'

Cornish leaned forward to read the first of the results on the screen:

The Evening Post
Wednesday, December 10th, 1947
A report by Stephen Jones

Putney Priest's Death Linked to Recent Child Abuse Case

The late Catholic priest, Father Shaun Thomas, who burnt to death three month's ago at his church in the borough of Putney, has become the subject of a child abuse case, after a number of the church's choristers came forward and reported him for sexual harassment.

Rumours are now circulating that Father Thomas's death might have been the result of a lone vigilante, seeking revenge, after a local resident recently reported seeing someone leaving the church only hours before his burnt remains were discovered.

Scotland Yard released a statement yesterday announcing that significant new evidence has recently emerged, and they are now treating the priest's death as suspicious.

The Evening Post can exclusively confirm that, as of this afternoon, Scotland Yard have instigated a murder enquirer into the death of Father Thomas.

Cornish rubbed the stubble on his chin. 'That's interesting, but I'm not sure it's got anything to do with Vera. Pull up the police file for that one just in case and send it to Melanie. I'll ask her to take a look at the details.'

'Okay,' ZeeZee replied.

Cornish continued to scan the list. 'What else have we got here, Maestro?'

Chapter 40

It was too quick and too painless, he thought

(York, 1970)

The old man was standing in the shadows when the front door opened. He watched intently as Phillip Manson stepped out into the rain and defiantly raised the collar of his jacket before locking the door and slipping the key under a large terracotta pot.

Manson was clearly much heavier now, compared to his day's at Llanarth Court, some twenty year's previous, and his lank hair was receding and thinning. He looked tired as he ambled down the road, struggling to light a cigarette in the wet and blustery conditions. 'Fucking weather!' he cursed as he walked.

The old man kept a good distance away but watched him until he entered the bar of the pub at the bottom of the hill. He then turned and limped back up the hill; his cap was pulled down over his face and his shoulders were hunched defiantly against the driving rain.

When he reached the end-of-terrace house he climbed the four steps, lifted the pot and picked up the key. He then quickly unlocked the front door and stepped inside. The hallway was dark and the place smelt of damp. The stairway, to his left, was dimly lit by a single bulb on the landing that gave off a pathetic yellow light.

He climbed the stairs quietly, and looked around. On his left was the bathroom that smelt of urine, in front of him was a closed door and to his right was another partly opened door. He walked towards it and peered in at a messy pile of cardboard boxes, a broken chair and an untidy pile of clothes. On top of one of the boxes he noticed a coiled up rope. He turned and walked back to the closed door on his right and something scurried across the landing.

'What the *fuck* was that?' he whispered.

When he pushed the door, it opened inwards, revealing a double bed in the middle of the room.

The old man glanced up at exposed beams where a large part of the ceiling had fallen down at some time in the past.

'Very convenient,' he said to himself.

Manson's bed was unmade and the sheets were creased and stained. An ashtray by the side of the bed was overflowing with cigarette ends. The stale smell was beginning to make him feel nauseous but he forced himself to enter the room.

Under the window, to his left, there was a chest of draws. He opened the top draw and gazed in. The sick images took his breath away and he raised his hand to his mouth; tears welled up in his eyes, blurring the explicit photos that made him retch with revulsion. He recognised the bed in the photographs as the dirty, stained bed he was now standing next to and he retched again. In his mind he could imagine the young frightened children being led up the stairs to the eager group of abusers.

More tears filled his eyes as he imagined the dire consequences of such a vile gathering. He envisaged the youngster, whimpering helplessly in the arms of an abuser. He looked at the stairs and imagined the child's flailing limbs and defiled body being carried down in the dark of night to the awaiting car. The car that would become the child's funeral hearse, transporting the still warm corpse, not to the cemetery, but to the woods, to be buried unceremoniously with the rest of them in the cold, damp earth.

Surely there is no greater evil on this earth? He thought as his resolve began to drain from his body.

When the old man arrived at the pub he placed his pipe in his mouth before pushing the door open into the smoky, public bar. He walked with slouched shoulders and made his way to the bar as rain water dripped off his cap onto the floorboards. He held a two shilling coin in his hand that quivered from the noticeable tremor that afflicted his hand and head and he asked the barmaid for a half of bitter.

The young girl poured the drink into a handle glass and placed it on the bar. 'That's a shilling please Mister,' she said, and took the coin from the stranger.

The old man quickly scanned the room and noticed Manson sitting alone at a table to his right, smoking a cigarette.

'Sir—your change,' the barmaid said.

'Thank you,' he mumbled and shuffled over to a table near the door. He pulled out a packet of St Bruno pipe tobacco from his coat pocket and filled his briar to the brim. He then struck a match and puffed contentedly on his pipe until the end glowed red; plumes of aromatic smoke surrounded him.

Manson, meanwhile, downed the dregs of his pint and walked up to the bar.

'Same again,' he said, and walked out through the door marked: TOILETS.

The old man quickly finished his half just as the barmaid placed Manson's fresh pint on the bar. He walked up to the counter and ordered another half. While the barmaid was pouring his drink he pulled a sachet from his pocket and deftly tipped the contents into Manson's beer.

Moments later Manson returned to the bar, picked up his pint and returned to his seat.

'Put it on my tab, love,' he said to the barmaid.

'You need to settle up this weekend,' she responded.

'Are you the new landlady then?' Manson asked.

'No,' she replied, defensively.

'No—that's right—because you're just a fucking barmaid, and don't you ever forget it?'

The old man puffed on his pipe and watched as Manson took a large slug of his pint.

The barmaid sneered at Manson. 'You're a *horrible* man. I don't why he let's you come in here.'

'Because my fucking money is as good as anyone else's—that's why—you cheeky little cow,' Manson replied.

'So how come we don't see any of it, then?'

'...A good fuck would sort you out,' Manson muttered under his breath as he sat down.

'What did you say?' the barmaid asked, but Manson just raised two fingers in defiance.

The old man had seen and heard enough. He finished his half, walked out of the pub and trudged back up the hill in the rain. In his pocket was the door key to Manson's house.

He opened the front door and then replaced the key under the pot before stepping into the house and closing the door behind him.

Forty minutes later the front door swung open with a thud as Manson fell into the hallway, groaning and slurring incomprehensibly. The old man watched him from the top of the stairs as he struggled to stand up. Eventually he forced himself into a standing position at the bottom of the stairs, only to fall forward and hit his chin on a stair riser. Blood and expletives poured from his mouth. Manson somehow made it to the top of the stairs, before staggering forward into his bedroom and falling heavily on the floor. More expletives followed before he quickly passed out.

The old man appeared in the doorway and smiled.

'You're back early,' he said, slipping his gloves on. He then tied one end of the rope around Manson's ankles and threw the other end over an exposed beam, which he then attached to the metal bed-frame that was now standing on-end up against the wall. He then pulled the bed until it fell forward and watched as Manson was yanked upwards; swinging unceremoniously upside down by his legs. Frothing vomit poured from his already bloodied mouth and nostrils, running down his face onto the bare floorboards.

'So far—so good,' he said, and walked over to the chest of draws. He picked up a long bladed kitchen knife before walking back and standing in front of Manson's upturned body. He calmly touched the soft fleshly jowl under his chin, and then, as Manson moaned unconsciously, he positioned the point of the knife blade midway between Manson's jaw bones and pushed until the knife point drew blood.

'This is payback time for all of those young, innocent lives you selfishly destroyed. It's such a shame you won't feel the pain like they did, or see the pleasure on my face—you fucking monster!'

And with that, he lunged the knife downwards through the roof of Manson's mouth, into his brain. He forcefully twisted the knife handle and watched excitedly as Manson's whole body convulsed in front of him like a performing marionette. A short-lived euphoria electrified the old man's senses; spoilt moments later by the acrid smell of urine running down his victim's now limp, lifeless body, adding to the already putrid stench in the room.

It was too quick and too painless, he thought, as he pulled the knife blade out of Manson's head.

Adrenalin was still surging through the old man's veins when he reached Lendal Bridge. He stopped there for a few minutes and leaned over the parapet, sensing, more than seeing the swollen River Ouse flowing below him in the darkness; then he hobbled the remaining ten minute walk back to his B&B at Gillygate.

The wet street was deserted when he approached his digs and the three-story-building was in darkness.

He quietly opened the front door and tiptoed his way up the stairs to his room on the first landing. Once inside the room, he locked the door and slipped the security chain into its holder. Exhausted, he leaned against the door, closed his eyes, and inhaled deeply through his nostrils. A moment later he exhaled slowly and stepped into the tiny en suite bathroom. He pulled on the light chord and stared in silence at the elderly man looking back at him from the wall mirror, but then he began to laugh out loud as he removed his cap and wig and carefully peeled off his beard.

Metamorphosed, Vera then removed her hairnet and shook her hair loose. Studiously, she moved closer to the mirror and with her finger she wiped a streak of blood off her forehead.

'It's time for a cigarette—and then—a long, *hot* bath my love,' she said, affectionately, to her own reflection. 'You deserve it.'

Chapter 41

A Senior Investigating Officer's worst nightmare

Melanie Underwood stepped on to the train at Cambridge Station and settled down at a window seat to re-read the Father Thomas file, sent to her by Senior Investigating Officer Ronnie Jarvis; the man she was meeting today for a *quid pro quo* lunch, as Jarvis had described it over the phone. The phrase had reminded her of Hannibal Lecter when he was skilfully negotiating with Officer Clarice Starling in *Silence of the Lambs.*

I hope he's not another Hannibal Lecter, she thought, as the disturbing image of the masked killer flashed into her mind. *Don't be silly girl, he might sound a bit slimy over the phone, but he's only a police officer—not a bloody cannibal!*

Melanie opened her briefcase and removed the beige file, marked:

Father Shaun Thomas—Case No. 144853-18-O.

Ronnie Jarvis had confirmed to her that the case was still open but no one in the London division was actively working on it due to the higher priority work-load pressures, and anyway, no new leads had emerged for years that would help the investigation.

She remembered his words:

'No resources are currently allocated to this low information investigation, which—naturally—I inherited, Miss Underwood.'

Melanie knew that *low information investigation* was police-speak for very little material to go on. No witnesses, no suspects, no fingerprints. A SIO's worst nightmare, according to Alan. She also had a very good idea why there were no clues to go on when she read Raymond (Porky) Bannister's statement to the police.

The train pulled into King's Cross Station on time and Melanie stepped down onto the platform and followed the instructions on her iPhone to the *Five Guys* restaurant on the corner of Pentonville Road, just a few minutes walk away.

'Whatever happened to tea at the Ritz?' she said, as she approached the restaurant. She noticed a guy smoking a cigarette outside the main entrance. He was wearing a black leather jacket, white shirt and tight jeans. He looked tanned and very fit.

As she approached, the man stubbed out his cigarette with his shoe. 'Miss Underwood?' he asked.

'Yes, that's me,' Melanie replied.

The man held out his hand. 'Ronnie Jarvis, pleased to meet you.'

Melanie shook his hand. 'Thanks for seeing me so promptly.'

'The pleasure's all mine, I can assure you, and please, call me Ronnie,' he said, with a smile that exposed his bleached teeth.

Oh God, thought Melanie, *as smooth as silk but a bit wrinkly around the edges, up close!*

Jarvis pushed on the entrance door. 'Let's go in, I'm starving,' he said, and gestured to Melanie to enter.

'I hope you don't mind my choice of restaurant?' he said, as they settled down at a window table overlooking Pentonville Road, 'but I'm hooked on their burgers.'

Melanie glanced at his slim physique and he noticed. 'Lot's of work-outs,' he said, tapping his six-pack. 'Do you work out, Miss Underwood?' he asked, with a cheeky smile.

'Call me Melanie.'

'Do you work out, Melanie?'

'I like to keep fit,' she replied.

'I can see that,' he said, with a smirk.

'Nice tan. Good holiday?' Melanie enquired, already anticipating the answer.

'Spray job, I'm afraid.'

'Fooled me,' she said.…'So—you are the SIO for the Father Thomas case.'

'That's right, I am. But, as I said to you over the phone, it's not at the top of my list of priorities at the moment. Too many knife and gun crimes to worry about, I'm afraid. So tell me—*why* is Probe so interested in the death of a priest that happened in nineteen-forty—?'

'Seven,' Melanie added.

'Yeah.'

'Because we believe that it's one of a number of *murders* committed by the *same* person.'

'Crime pattern analysis—Subject profile analysis?' Jarvis asked.

'Exactly! I'm studying profiling as part of my PhD studies in Criminal Psychology. Motivational drivers, predictive policing, that sort of thing.'

'It's all the rage at the moment, this predictive policing.'

'Yes, I believe so,' Melanie agreed.

'So—you're not just a pretty face then?'

Melanie managed a smile.

'Have you got a suspect?' Jarvis asked.

'Jessica Whatley, aka Vera Parsons; and she's still alive.'

'Any evidence?'

Melanie shook her head. 'Nothing to convict her.'

'All premeditated then.'

'Yeah—unfortunately.'

'The SIO's nightmare,' Jarvis added.

Melanie nodded. 'Yes, I know. I'm familiar with the CPIA.'

'The Criminal Procedures and Investigations Act. That's another thing that gives me fucking nightmares! And you're familiar with it , you say?' Jarvis sounded dubious.

'Reasonably, yes,' Melanie answered.

Jarvis leaned forward. 'So what are the three offences included in the Home Office definition of homicide?'

'Murder, manslaughter and infanticide,' Melanie responded.

'Homicide investigations typically have two distinct and strategic phases, what are they?' Jarvis asked.

Melanie looked him in the eyes and smiled. 'It's *three* phases actually: instigation, investigation and case management; Brookman, 2005, Understanding Homicide.'

Jarvis pulled back, open-mouthed. '...That's fucking impressive! So, what *exactly* do you want from me, Melanie?'

'I want *your* permission to speak to one of *your* witnesses.'

'Tell me more?'

'In his statement he says that he was *urged* to come forward to the police by his best friend; a girl named Jess. I believe the *Jess* he was referring to is actually Jessica Whatley.'

'Aka Vera Parsons?'

'Precisely!'

'And who is this witness?' Jarvis asked.

'A chap named Roger *Porky* Bannister. We did a trace on him and he's living in north London.'

A waitress arrived to take their food order but Jarvis waved her away. 'So what was Jessica Whatley's motive for killing Father Thomas?'

'Simple—Father Thomas was a paedophile, and as a child, Jessica Whatley had suffered year's of sexual abuse by her perverted stepfather. So much so that she killed him with a red-hot poker rammed into his eye socket. Father Thomas was just another pervert to get rid of because Jessica knew he'd been sexually abusing the members of his choir—but more importantly, she knew he'd been abusing her best friend, Porky Bannister, because he'd admitted it to her. So, in retribution, she burnt the priest on the fire. That's my *hypothesis* anyway! Incidentally, years later, she killed her *paedophile* half-brother because he'd stabbed her lover through the heart with a kitchen knife.'

'Fuck me!' Jarvis exclaimed.

No thank you, Melanie thought, *you're definitely not my type.*

'Sounds to me like you've gone un opened Pandora's Box.'

'But the last thing to leave Pandora's Box was what?' Melanie asked.

'Dunno,' said Jarvis.

'Hope,' Melanie replied.

'Christ! Is there anything you don't know?'

'Too much at the moment, unfortunately,' Melanie responded.

'…So, the person seen leaving the church on the night of the murder by this caretaker woman, Florence —what's her name?'

'Florence Atkins; she was the one who found the priest's remains.'

'Yeah, that's her, Akins. So it was Jessica Whatley she saw leaving the church.'

'Most likely,' Melanie agreed, 'but it's impossible to prove it, of course.'

'But she would have been just a kid!' Jarvis said.

'She was just a kid when she killed her stepfather,' Melanie added.

Jarvis looked pensive…'Well—I have no objection to you speaking with this Porky Bannister chap. But I'm not sure what it'll actually achieve. Just keep me in the loop, okay?'

'Thank you, I will,' Melanie replied.

'Shall we eat?' Jarvis waved to the waitress.

'What do you recommend?' Melanie asked.

'I'm going for a burger, but beware, they are a *big* mouthful!'

'Oh good, I like a *big* mouthful,' Melanie answered, and watched as Jarvis's cool demeanour crumbled in front of her eyes.

'Two specials,' Jarvis said to the waitress when she approached their table.

'Any drinks, guys?' she asked.

'Full-fat Coke for me and—?'

'Regular latte for me, please,' Melanie replied.

When the waitress had gone, Jarvis said:

'…Give my regards to Alan when you see him, won't you.'

Melanie looked surprised. 'You *know* Alan Cornish?'

'Yeah—not well, but we've bumped into each other over the years: police conferences, dinners, that sort of thing. Bloody good copper he was, good looking chap too; always had the girls chasing after him. What about you Melanie—ave you got a fella?'

'…Yeah—as a matter of fact—I have.'

'I fort yer might, good-looker like you. If I was Cornish I'd ave *real* trouble keeping my hands off you, I can tell yer.'

Melanie smiled. '…Alan doesn't have to.'

Ronnie Jarvis looked perplexed. 'What do you mean?'

'…He doesn't have to keep his hands off me.'

Jarvis swallowed hard.

Melanie leaned forward for effect and said:

'I'll be honest with you, Ronnie, I'm a fucking nymphomaniac… And it's the *best* sex I've ever had. As I said to you before—I like a *big* mouthful!'

Ronnie Jarvis's jaw dropped and his blood pressure surged.

Chapter 42

Champagne at the bloody Waldorf!

'You might have warned me, Alan,' Melanie said, striding into Cornish's office.

Cornish looked up from his desk and grinned. 'How was Ronnie?'

'He's a slime bag! But you knew that, didn't you!'

'I was *confident* you'd be able to handle the likes of him,' Cornish said, calmly. 'More importantly, did you get what you wanted?'

'Yes, I did. I've arranged to visit this Porky Bannister chap to talk to him about his statement. His daughter said that he's suffering from signs of early dementia, but his long-term memory is still good.'

'Excellent, well done.'

Melanie walked over to Cornish and kissed him on the lips. 'You bastard!' she said, with a smile.

'Good lunch?' he asked.

'Exquisite! He took me to the Waldorf. It must have cost him a small fortune, what with the cocktails and the bottle of Veuve Clicquot as well.'

'What!' Exclaimed Cornish, flaring his nostrils. '*Champagne* at the bloody *Waldorf*!'

'Yeah, but I'm worth it,' she said,… 'Ronnie told me so. I just wish I'd worn a more revealing top, because I have a feeling Ronnie's a *breast* man and he would have *loved* my cleavage. That was definitely an opportunity missed!' she said, as she strutted out of the office biting her bottom lip.

Chapter 43

She should be honoured not harassed

'What the hell were you on last night?' Melanie asked as she drained the poached eggs in the kitchen sink.

'What do you mean?' Cornish asked as he pulled up a chair at the breakfast table.

'My thighs are bruised,' Melanie said.

'Sorry,' he said, 'I was in the mood.'

'You're not kidding. I feel knackered this morning.'

'Sorry,' Cornish repeated.

'I'm not complaining,' she said, and leaned over to kiss him.

'What time are you seeing this, Porky, guy?'

'Ten-thirty, in Enfield,' she answered and placed their breakfasts of poached eggs and crispy bacon on the table.

'That looks lovely,' Cornish said.

'You'll need that to build your strength back up after last night's performance, Rasputin.'

Cornish chuckled at her comment. 'When you came back to the office and told me about your lunch date with Jarvis, I felt so jealous. And your comment about your cleavage worked me up into a lather.'

Melanie moved close to Cornish and lifted her top. 'But you know they're all yours and nobody else's, don't you?' she said, as she guided her nipple into his mouth.

It was 10.48 when Melanie arrived at the large detached house near Enfield. As she parked her Mini on the drive the front door of the house opened and a smiling middle-aged woman greeted her with a wave. Melanie exited the car and walked over to the lady. 'You must be Sally?' she asked.

'And you must be Melanie?'

'Yes, sorry I'm a little late but I was unexpectedly delayed this morning.' *That sounds more acceptable than saying I was having wild sex on the kitchen table for twenty minutes,* she thought to herself.

'It's not a problem, Melanie. Dad isn't going anywhere in a hurry. Come in and I'll put the kettle on.'

Ohhhh, I could murder a cup of tea. 'Thanks Sally, that's very kind of you.'

Once inside the house Sally closed the front door. 'Miss Underwood is here, Dad,' she called out.

'Who?' came the reply from the living room.

'Miss Underwood.' Sally repeated.

'Who's that?'

'What exactly is it you want to see Dad about Melanie?' Sally asked as she filled the kettle in the sink.

'It's nothing for you or your Dad to worry about Sally, but I'm investigating a lady who was possibly a friend of your Dad's when they were young.'

'So why are you investigating this lady now? That was a long time ago, wasn't it?' Sally asked.

Melanie hesitated. '…Well, I can't tell you the exact details of the case but we think she might have been involved in a murder.'

'Oh my God!'

'Please, don't fret. Your Dad is not involved in any way, other than he may have known her as a friend when they were young. I just want to confirm one way or another that it's the same woman.' Melanie recalled Porky's statement and how he loved the milk and biscuits when he visited Jessica. 'Can I ask a favour of you, Sally?'

'Yes, what can I do for you?'

'Could I have a glass of milk and some biscuits, please?'

'Skipped breakfast did we, young lady?' Sally obliged. 'You'd better come through then,' she said, and walked into the sunny living room. Porky was sitting in an armchair looking out through the double-glazed sliding doors at the familiar view onto the sun terrace. He was wearing large-framed glasses with think lenses and his ginger hair was now as white as snow, but it was still as thick as when he was a skinny lad in Putney.

'Dad, this is Melanie, she's come to ask you some questions, all right?'

'Melanie, yeah,' he said, somewhat confused.

'Hello Mister Bannister,' Melanie said, and held out her hand.

'Melanie,' he said, ignoring her hand and staring out of the window with a frown.

'Mister Bannister, I'd like to ask you about your time in Putney.'

'Putney, yeah,' he said, and smiled.

'Do you remember Putney, Mister Bannister?'

'Putney—yeah.'

'Do you remember your best friend, Mister Bannister?'

'My best friend—yeah—I remember her.'

Melanie asked: 'What was her name?'

'You was my best friend.'

'What was her name, Dad?' his daughter interjected.

'It's Jess, of course—Jess. She was my best friend, weren't yer.'

'What was her surname, Dad?'

The old man looked hard into the distance. 'I was in love with yer. All the boys said that it was you who killed that dirty priest but they didn't know anyfing. You got very angry when you found out what he'd done to me, didn't yer, Jess?' Porky said, looking at Melanie.

The phone in the hall began to ring and Sally excused herself to answer it.

Melanie waited a moment. 'Have a biscuit Porky?' she said quietly.

'Fanks Jess,' the old man said with a smile. 'Where yer bin then, girl?'

'I had to go away, didn't I?' Melanie answered.

'I never told anyone, Jess,' he said, biting into the biscuit.

'About what Porky?'

'You knows—about the priest—you, killing him for what he'd done to me.'

'Did you see me kill the priest, Porky?'

'You knows I didn't Jess. You went on yer own didn't yer? ...Can I have my milk now, Jess?'

251

'Yeah,' Melanie said, and gave the old man the glass.

'Nobody saw nuffin and nobody cun prove anyfing. One of the boys in the choir said you dunnit Jess, but he didn't no nuffing really and he kept it quiet, cos I told him if he said anyfing I'd burn him on the fire too. You don't 'ave to worry girl, I never told 'em our secret.' The old man tapped the side of his nose with his finger.

'Thank you Porky.'

'I loved yer I did, and then you just up and left me, just like that. But you always promised to come back and see me, didn't yah girl?'

Melanie reached out and held the old man's hand just as Sally walked back into the room.

'Sorry about that,' she said. '...Has Dad taken your milk?' she asked.

'Don't worry about it.'

'Dad! That was Melanie's milk.'

'I knew you'd come back,' he muttered to himself and took a sip from the glass.

Back in the kitchen, Sally confronted Melanie. 'You don't expect my Dad to go to court do you, as a witness?'

'No, I don't, Sally. Please don't worry, that won't happen. I needed to confirm that this Jess in Putney was the same person as the one we're currently investigating and thankfully your Dad did that. I'm very grateful to the both of you.'

'So what will happen to this Jessica woman now?'

'Probably nothing; we have no evidence to convict her.'

'What did Dad know?'

'He confirmed it was the same person but he never actually witnessed the incident.'

'…Is it possible that they could meet again?'

They just did, Melanie thought. 'I'm not sure Sally. That would be up to Vera, I suppose.'

'Who's Vera?'

'Sorry—that's Jessica—she's now known as Vera Parsons. But in all honesty, if they did meet I don't think your Dad would recognise her. His memories of her are locked in his childhood past. Jess is an old lady now, and truthfully, your dad wouldn't recognise her.'

'So this Jess woman killed a priest because he was a paedophile?'

'Yes, we believe she did,' Melanie answered.

'Well, I think she should be honoured not harassed.'

'She's not being harassed, Sally. She's playing a game with us and thoroughly enjoying it too.'

Sally asked:

'The church is full of bloody perverts, and they protect them, too. It makes my blood boil! If you had the evidence would you convict her for killing a *paedophile*?'

Melanie managed a tight-lipped smile. '…That's a tough call. I'm a psychologist not a detective, but you can't condone murder under any circumstances, can you? That's why we have laws.'

Sally responded:

'Well, having three kids of my own, I can tell you now I wouldn't convict her; I'd give her a bloody medal instead!'

Melanie smiled sympathetically. *I'm beginning to think the same way,* she thought. 'If you don't mind, Sally, I'll say goodbye to your Dad and I'll make my way back to the office.'

'Have you got far to go?' Sally asked.

'Only Cambridge; straight up the M11.'

'Not far then? Dad! Melanie's going now; say goodbye to her, please.'

When Melanie walked into the lounge the empty milk glass was rolling across the floor and Porky was slumped in his chair with his head to the side.

Melanie called out, 'Oh, Sally, I'm so sorry!'

Chapter 44

And she did—and he died a happy man

When Melanie returned to the office she looked exhausted. Her eyes were red and puffy and she flopped into her chair at her desk.

Cornish noticed her arriving and hurried over to see her. When she saw him she burst into tears.

'What's happened?' he asked, putting his hand on her shoulder. 'Have you had an accident? I tried ringing you but you didn't answer.'

'No, I'm okay, Alan.'

'You don't look okay.'

'Porky *died* in the fucking house, when I was there!'

'Oh dear, that's awful! I think you need a coffee, my love.'

'Make it a strong one, please,' she replied.

Thirty minutes later Melanie was sitting in Cornish's office recalling the conversation she had with Porky.

'He confirmed it to me,' she said, and wiped her eyes with a tissue. 'It was Jessica Whatley, just as I suspected. She killed the priest because he was a paedophile, messing with the boys in the choir and Porky was one of them. It was Porky that alerted her to the priest's disgusting habits. But nobody actually saw her kill Father Thomas.'

'My God!' Cornish exclaimed. 'How many *others* has she killed?'

'There is a common theme here, isn't there?'

Cornish nodded. 'Yeah, and as far as we know she *only* kills paedophiles. Some people might consider her a hero.'

'Yes, as a matter of fact I met one today.'

'Who was that?'

'Porky's daughter; she said she deserved a bloody medal!'

'…You look a bit better now,' he said. 'You looked awful when you got back. I felt so sorry for you, but I was so glad to see you. I was really worried about you.'

Melanie smiled. 'I wasn't expecting that, Alan… Porky thought I was Jess. He told me he loved me and that he knew I'd come back to see him one day… It was as if he'd been waiting all this time for Jess to turn up.' Tears welled up in Melanie's eyes.

'And she did—and he died a happy man,' Cornish said, as Melanie broke down in a flood of tears again.

'Do you want to tell Vera?'

Melanie pulled a tissue from her sleeve and blew her nose, struggling to compose herself. '…Yes, I think she ought to know that Porky has died…and I think she ought to know that we know she killed the priest, too.'

'Will you arrange to go and see her?'

'Yes, I will, but it won't be today.'

'I'll come with you when you go; just as long as it's not raining. I can't do this boiled cabbage and stale piss thing!'

Melanie giggled for the first time that day. 'She'll be delighted to see you again, h*andsome!*'

Cornish smiled. '…I *really* love you, you know that don't you?'

'I know you do—and I really love you too, *Rasputin*! Hold me please, …hold me tight.'

'…And *never* let you go,' Cornish whispered in her ear, as he wrapped his arms around her.

Chapter 45

We were just kids

'The forecast is twenty-four-degrees and sunny.'

'That's good news,' Cornish replied to Melanie who was leaning around his office door. 'What time's our appointment with Vera then?'

'She's expecting us around three-thirty.'

'So there's no lunch with her today then?'

'No, she's not back until one o'clock. She's on a trip to a National Trust garden somewhere in the country. I've got her some chocolates though.'

'Good idea,' replied Cornish as his desk phone rang.

He hit the speaker button and answered the call coming from reception.

'I've got a Bill Morrison on the line. He wants to speak to you, Alan.'

'Put him through please, Sarah…Bill?'

'Yes, good morning, Alan.'

'How are you, Bill?'

'Fine thanks, Alan, and you?'

'Yeah good…What can I do for you today.'

'It's more like what I can do for you, I think.'

'Oooh, please tell me more.'

'I was in the office the other day and I was chatting with my old mate Alex the stores manager; we play golf together you see. I asked him if I could have a wander around because something was bugging me. He let me in, and I'm glad he did, because I found something, but not where it was supposed to be.'

'What did you find, Bill?'

'I found the rope that Manson had been strung up with!'

'Where is it now?'

'It's still in its sealed bag on the desk in front of me. The SIO here has said that I can ship it to you; as long as it's treated as possible evidence and won't be contaminated.'

'Send it straight to Christopher Copeland, please. He'll deal with it; do you have his address?'

'Yes, we've dealt with them before,' Morrison confirmed.

'This is good news, Bill.'

'I've been thinking of you and the problems you're having solving this case. This might just give you something to go on.'

'Let's hope so, Bill. I'll give Christopher a call now and make sure he's expecting it. Thank you so much for your help.'

'It's my pleasure, Alan. I'll speak with you again sometime. Goodbye.'

'Goodbye.' Cornish hit the end-call button and headed off to the coffee machine tapping his fingers together.

Melanie saw him and when he noticed her he gestured to her to join him.

When she arrived he said:

'I've just been talking to Bill Morrison, remember him?'

'Yes, I remember him—retired SIO. So what did he want?'

'He's only gone and found the rope that Vera tied Manson up with, and it's still in its sealed evidence bag.'

'That rope could prove that Vera was actually there.'

'Yes, it could, if we get lucky and find her DNA on it; and if she wasn't wearing gloves at the time that could be a *very* strong possibility.'

'Would it be enough to convict her?' Melanie asked.

'With a good prosecution lawyer, yes, I think it might be possible. But let's not jump the gun; Vera's a smart cookie, as you well know.'

'Yes, I know,' replied Melanie, thoughtfully.

Vera was sitting on the garden bench enjoying the glorious weather when Melanie and Alan arrived and she waved to them as they crossed the lawn.

'Hello Vera,' Melanie called out as they approached.

'Hello my dear, hello handsome,' she replied.

Cornish smiled. 'Hello Vera, how are you today?'

'Enjoying the weather,' she replied.

'It's glorious isn't it,' said Melanie, as she slipped next to Vera on the bench.' How was your visit to the gardens?'

Ignoring the question she said:

'Oh, chocolates, are they for me my dear?'

'Yes, Vera, they're for you.'

'Thank you, you're very kind,' she said, placing the box on her lap.

'Vera, I'm sorry to tell you but I have some sad news for you,' Melanie said.

'Sad news, what sad news?'

'It concerns your childhood friend, Porky.'

'What about him?' Vera asked, anxiously. 'What about Porky?'

'…Porky passed away two day's ago,Vera… I'm very sorry.'

Vera remained silent for some time. Finally, she turned to Melanie and asked:

'How do you know about Porky?'

'We know that you and Porky were childhood friends. I was there when he passed away, Vera. Before he died he told me that he loved you.'

Vera shook her head. '…We were just *kids*. We didn't know what *love* was then—but we trusted each other and we cared for each other, that's what mattered. But it wasn't love… How come *you* were there when he died?' Vera asked.

Melanie glanced at Alan.

'Were you there to find out if I killed the priest?'

'…Yes,' replied Melanie.

'He tried to finger me when I went to see him,' she said. 'He made me feel sick.'

Cornish raised his hand to his mouth.

'I had to kill him, he was a monster. There, are you happy now? …Are you going to arrest me?' Vera asked.

No, we're not going to arrest you, Vera, Cornish answered.

'But I just *confessed* to a murder.'

'That's not *evidence* that you killed him, Vera,' replied Cornish. You've told us things before that weren't true.

'But I did kill him. I stabbed him in the heart with a kitchen knife and threw him on the fire. I can still smell his burning flesh. He abused Porky and that was like abusing me. So I had to kill him—I had no choice.'

'Is that why you killed your half-brother, Vera?'

Vera sighed heavily. 'I've only ever done what I thought was right. There are a lot of *bad* people in this world, you know, evil people, with no *feelings* for others. These people exist just to satisfy their own stinking, perverted needs. They are happy to destroy innocent people's lives just as long as they can satisfy their own disgusting lusts. Believe me, I know, because I've been on the receiving end far too often—and quite frankly, these *monsters* deserve to die.'

Vera glanced at Cornish, and noticed he was nodding at Vera in agreement.

Chapter 46

I think I might know how to get her to tell us

'She knows that we can't do *anything* about it. Her confession to us is nothing more than showmanship; she's playing with us, as usual,' Cornish said, before finishing his beer. He waved to the waitress and ordered another pint and another glass of wine for Melanie. 'I love sitting by the river,' he said.

'I know you do,' she said, and smiled affectionately. 'Has Christopher received the rope yet?' Melanie asked.

'Yes, he has, but they can't do anything this week because of their current work load. But that will be interesting if we get a result.'

Melanie pondered:

'I wonder how Vera will react if we really do obtain evidence to convict her?'

'How will you react?' Cornish asked.

'I must admit, I have mixed emotions, Alan. I noticed you nodding in agreement with Vera.'

'Do you know something, love, I tried to put myself in Vera's position and surprisingly, I felt empathy for her and for the first time I could understand where she was coming from.'

'I felt the same way,' Melanie said.

'What we have to do now, love, is evaluate the hypothesis that Vera may well have killed Weldon.'

'We need to find her *motive*—but that won't be easy.'

'Let's be honest, none of this has been easy Melanie, has it?' Cornish added. 'The *obvious* hypothesis, based on crime pattern analysis, is that Vera killed Weldon because he was a paedophile. So I'll get Zeezee on the case and see what he can dig up about the doctor's past. But, if the rope turns out to be clean then our investigation, to date, has proved *nothing*! And somehow I don't think Vera is going to tell us who killed Weldon.'

'I think I might know how to get her to tell us,' Melanie said, and finished her glass of wine.

'Really! Tell me more,' Cornish asked, excitedly.

Chapter 47

Once again, it's been a real pleasure doing business with you Doctor

(Llanarth Court, August 1952)

A ripple of excitement washed over Vera's body as Weldon kissed her neck, tenderly, and his wandering hand found its way into her knickers.

'No time for that now, love. I'm on duty in ten minutes, I'm afraid,' Vera said, checking her watch.

'Tonight then?—Shall we have a session?' Weldon suggested, excitedly.

'To be honest I was expecting you to go down the pub with your drinking partner.'

'What about when I get back from the pub then?'

'I'm sorry Tony but I'll be fast asleep by then and you'll be very drunk; but I'm sure you'll enjoy the evening with your *best* friend.'

Weldon sighed. '…The poor sod's had a real bad infection in his hand. He hasn't been at all well these last few days.'

'How did he do that?' Vera asked, coolly.

'Not sure really; I couldn't get much sense out of him when I asked him about it. I gave him some cream for it and it seems to have done the trick. It looked to me as if he'd been stabbed with a fork, of all things!'

'Do you intend to keep him?' Vera asked, coldly.

'No—he's not what I was hoping for—his bedside manner is not the best and his initial enthusiasm has most definitely worn off.'

Vera smiled and punched the air. 'So when are you getting rid of him?'

'After his six week's probation period is up. He's got another two weeks to go.' Weldon explained.

'Does he know he's leaving?'

'No, he doesn't, but I'll have to tell him at some point in the near future.'

Vera kissed Weldon and said:

'I've *never* liked him, you know that… I'm off now, see you tomorrow,' she said, and walked out.

'Yeah—I'll see you tomorrow, sexy,' Weldon said as Vera closed the door behind her.

Ten minutes later there was a knock on Weldon's door. Weldon checked his watch and smiled. 'Come in,' he said.

As the door opened he asked:

'How's your hand?'

Manson smiled and said:

'I'll survive.'

'Turn the key in the lock.'

Manson locked the door and then placed his briefcase on Weldon's bed.

'What have you got for me this time?' Weldon asked, excitedly.

Manson opened his briefcase and took out a brown envelope. 'Take a look at these,' he said, passing the envelope to Weldon.

Weldon's hands were trembling as he opened the envelope and pulled out the photographs... 'Fucking hell!' he said. 'These are the best yet. How much for these, Phillip?'

'There's twenty of them all together and they're a couple of quid each.'

'Expensive!'

'Not for that kind of material, Tony.'

'Yeah, that's true. And they're so young too,' Weldon said, breathing erratically.

Manson smiled. 'You told me the *younger* the better.'

'Yeah I know; you've done well Phillip.'

Manson smiled. 'And now that I've set up a regular supply they'll all be of this high quality in future. Do you want more next month?'

'...Ye...Yeah of course I do!' Weldon said, engrossed in the images. He opened his bedside draw and pulled out a bundle of one-pound notes and counted out forty quid onto the bed in four piles of ten.

Manson gathered up the notes, slipped them into his jacket pocket and closed his briefcase. 'Once again, it's been a real pleasure doing business with you Doctor,' he said, smirking. 'See you tonight for a few pints?'

'Yeah, I look forward to it.'

Manson picked up his briefcase, unlocked the door and walked out of the room, closing the door behind him.

Weldon rushed to the door and quickly turned the key in the lock. His hands were trembling with excitement as he picked up the first photograph. 'You *dirty* fucking bitch,' he whispered, fumbling to undo the buttons of his flies.

Chapter 48

The results of our tests found over forty different
kinds of DNA

(Copeland and Associates, Huntington)

'**Good afternoon** both,' Christopher Copeland said, when he walked into reception.

'Hi Christopher,' Cornish replied, getting to his feet and shaking hands with Copeland.

'How are you my dear?' Copeland asked Melanie and kissed her on the cheek.

'Very well, thank you, Christopher,' she replied, 'It's lovely to see you again.'

'Melanie, I can *assure* you, the pleasure is all mine. Come on through,' he said, and tapped a security code into the keypad next to the internal door. 'I've got some fresh coffee and chocolate Hobnobs on my desk. As usual Alan—no expense spared,' he joked.

Cornish laughed. 'Don't hold out your hopes for a biscuit, Melanie. We're talking Christopher and chocolate Hobnobs here!'

Copeland laughed out loud and opened the door to the office. He gestured to Melanie and Copeland to enter and said:

'Make yourselves comfortable and please pour out the coffee. I'll go and get Anne who did the tests on the rope.'

Moments later Copeland returned with a young lady. She was wearing a white coat and hanging around her neck was her identity badge which along with her photo carried the label: Anne Sellors—Senior Laboratory Technician.

'Anne, this is Alan and Melanie from Probe,' Copeland said. 'They her to find out the results of the tests you did on the rope.'

Anne said hello and shook hands with Copeland and Melanie. She then asked Copeland if she could access her data from his desktop computer.

'It's all yours,' he said to Anne, and settled on a chair next to Melanie.

'Please bear with me a moment,' she said, then started typing. A few moments later she smiled and said:

'Okay, I've got the results here.'

Melanie glanced at Cornish and he winked at her.

'I must say this was one of the most difficult tests that I have ever conducted. The rope was actually twenty-two-feet long,' Anne Sellors emphasised, 'and when you're looking for microscopic clues it feels like twenty-two-*miles!* I can tell you.'

Come on come on, get on with it! Melanie thought.

'The results of our tests found over forty different kinds of DNA, mostly human, but some animal DNA also. For example we identified rat, cat and dog DNA. We ran the comparison tests on the human DNA and checked them against Vera's DNA and,' Anne Sellors paused for effect.

Get on with it! Melanie screamed in her head.

'The results showed no matches. In other words Vera's DNA was not present on the rope.'

Melanie struggled to hold back a smile. She felt a strange sense of relief when she heard the results of the test. I should be disappointed, but I'm not, she thought.

'I can't say I'm surprised,' Cornish said, 'Vera's not one for leaving us clues,' he said, looking at Copeland.

'Thank you Anne,' Copeland said, 'you can get back to your other duties now.'

'Yeah, thank you very much Anne,' Cornish added, as she said her goodbyes and left the office.

Cornish sipped his coffee and accepted a Hobnob from Copeland. '…This woman has beaten the system. She has killed numerous people and she's got away with it.'

'Well, you gave it your best shot, Alan! You knew the odds were against you at the start.'

'When I first met Vera I asked her what had happened on that fateful night when her lover was killed. She said to me what do you care, you weren't even born then. And ever since then the answer to that question has haunted me. I *need* to know what happened and it's now time to implement my plan.'

'What plan is that?' asked Copeland.

'Well, it's obvious isn't it?' Melanie replied with a wry smile.

Chapter 49

That's the deal

Vera Parsons looked up at the London Eye in awe. 'Are we really going up there, Melanie?' she asked, excitedly.

'Yes, we are Vera, the views of the city from up there are amazing. You can see the sights of London so clearly. Are you happy to do it?'

'I can't wait!' she said.

'Come on then let's go, Melanie said, offering Vera her arm.'

'Are you coming too, handsome?' Vera asked.

'I wouldn't miss it for the world, Vera,' Cornish replied.

Melanie handed the tickets to the attendant and then helped Vera into the pod. Vera settled on a bench seat flanked by Cornish and Melanie. 'How exciting,' she said, gripping her handbag tightly, 'I never thought I'd do this, my dear; I'm so grateful to you both.'

'We're lucky with the weather today; the views are going to be stunning, Vera,' Cornish enthused. 'The breeze has cleared away the morning mist.'

'It's good when the mist clears, isn't it?' Melanie said, looking at Vera.

'Are you going to tell me what you've found then, young lady?' Vera asked bluntly, 'or do I have to wait until we get to the top?'

Melanie smiled as the pod started to move. 'We have found the rope, Vera.'

Vera nodded a tight-lipped smile.

'Do you know what DNA is Vera?'

'I've heard of it, dear, but I don't know what it is.'

Melanie took Vera's hand. 'It's a chemical set of instructions that makes you what you are. Your DNA is *unique* Vera, it's in nearly every cell of your body. No one else's DNA is like yours and if we find your DNA on something, it means that you have been in contact with it.'

Vera looked at Melanie. 'Like the rope?'

'Yes, we found DNA on the rope. DNA evidence is enough to convict someone of murder.'

Vera fell silent.

Melanie glanced at Cornish who winked at her.

'Are you going to arrest me?' she asked.

'That all depends on you, Vera,' Cornish responded.

'What do you want from me?' Vera asked.

'The truth about who killed Tony Weldon,' Melanie said, emphatically.

'If I tell you, will you arrest me?'

'No, Vera, we just want to know what happened.'

'That's the deal,' Cornish added.

'Okay—by the time we reach the top, you'll know exactly who killed Tony,' she said, and removed a handkerchief from her sleeve.

Chapter 50

It's so clear now, isn't it?

'I'd been suspicious of my half-brother for some time. He'd got into a relationship with Sally Griffith—one of the nurses at Llanarth. He was just using her of course, that's the kind of man he was. Sally had become hooked on morphine and was stealing it from the medical stores. Roger—Manson—whatever *you* want to call him, saw it as an opportunity and very quickly he'd set up a supply chain to his contacts in London. He was making a lot of money selling high grade morphine; and Sally was on the take too and cooking the books. I told Tony about it and he said that the situation was intolerable and that he would have to get rid of the both of them. I remember the feeling of sheer elation, knowing that Roger was going to be removed from the premises. It felt as if I was finally going to get my life back.' Vera sighed and then took a deep breath. 'One afternoon I was in my room when

Roger knocked on my door. He looked angry and said that Tony wanted to see me urgently in his office. I made my way down there and he followed behind me in stony silence. I knocked on Tony's door but Roger just pushed it open and then he pushed me in. Tony was sitting at his desk when I entered, but then I noticed there was blood on his chest. I turned and saw Sally Griffith who sank a syringe into my neck. I remember her saying, "Take that you bitch!" and then I passed out. When I came around I was alone, lying on top of Tony's body.'

'Oh Vera!' Melanie groaned.

'I knew that I'd been set up, but I wasn't going to hang for something I didn't do. My only thoughts were those of revenge—and eventually I achieved my goal.'

'And liver cancer killed Sally Griffith, didn't it Alan?' Melanie said.

'That's right, it did, quite a few years ago now,' he replied.

Vera smiled, contentedly. '…It wasn't the cancer that killed her,' she said, confidently.

Melanie looked at Cornish, who raised his eyebrows.

Vera continued. 'It's true that Sally Griffith terminally ill, but what *actually* killed her was a massive overdose of morphine, expertly administered in a hospice near Abergavenny,' Vera explained, as she stood up and walked over to look at the panoramic views, now that their pod neared the top of the wheel. Vera grabbed the handrail with both hands. '... Thankfully, even though she was dying, she was able to recognise me, even though I was dressed as a nun when I walked into Room Fourteen. Hello Sally, I said, and I watched her as her frightened eyes followed my every move. I can still see the fear on her face as if it was yesterday when she mumbled my name. Then she asked me if I'd come to kill me? I stood over her ailing body, smiling at her, and I said—It's only what you deserve. Then I emptied my syringe into her neck—just like she'd done to me all those years ago when she robbed me of the only man I'd ever loved, and ruined my beautiful dreams, forever... The last words—no— the last *well-chosen* words Sally Griffith ever heard were *mine*.'

Vera became quietly pensive—reliving the moment when she'd emptied the syringe into Sally Griffith's neck and sneered into her victim's eyes as the life began to drain from her body.

'Take that you bitch!' she'd said, as her victim's breath finally failed her.

Vera allowed herself a wry smile as a rare rush of adrenalin surged through her veins. She turned to face Melanie and Tony and said:

'So you see, it wasn't me who killed Tony…I loved him dearly. He was the only man I have ever really loved. Oh—just look at the beautiful view!' she suddenly enthused.

'It's so clear now, isn't it?' a tearful Melanie said to Cornish, as she gave Vera an emotional hug.

'It's so nice to feel alive again, my dear,' Vera said, and kissed Melanie on her cheek. Turning to Tony she said:

'And remember what I told you, handsome, don't leave it too long.'

'I won't, I promise, Vera,' Cornish replied, and gently hugged her frail body.

Melanie thought back to the time when she first met Vera; the cantankerous and capricious old lady at the nursing home. *Of all the explanations for that fateful day, I wasn't expecting that!*

Cornish said:

'This time Vera, I think we've finally got to the truth.'

Vera smiled and said:

'Would I lie to you, handsome?'

Melanie's iPhone rang in her jacket and she pulled it out; the display said it was ZeeZee calling.

'Excuse me a moment,' she said, and turned away. 'Hi, ZeeZee, what's up?'

'Hi Melanie, I've been doing some more digging, and I've unearthed a transcript from the mental institution where Vera was banged up. It's dated 1969 —that's just a year before her release.'

Melanie was immediately interested. 'What does it say?' she asked.

ZeeZee continued:

'Well, most of it's pretty uninteresting stuff, to be honest, but during one conversation that Vera had with a nurse, she admitted that shortly before Weldon's death—and I quote—*"I found a file in his office which contained photographs that ripped out my heart."*'

— The End —

Thank you for reading 'Shroud The Truth With Silence.' If you would like details of my other novels or wish to contact me, please visit my website at:

haydnjones-author.com

Other novels by this author include:

- The Angels of Destiny
- The Devil and the Unicorn
- The Journal of Harry Somerville

16630440R00169

Printed in Great Britain
by Amazon